MW01153852

Cathy,
We all
wear
masks!

Unmask

Adrenaline Series 4

By Xavier Neal

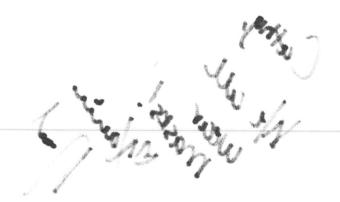

Unmask

Adrenaline Series 4

By Xavier Neal

© Xavier Neal 2015

Published by Entertwine Publishing

Cover by Entertwine Publishing

Photographer: Xavier Neal

All Rights Reserved

ISBN-13:
978-1517621421

ISBN-10:
1517621429

Dedicated To The Universe: Thank you for letting me take off my mask over a decade ago.

Drew

With a wide yawn, I carefully peel away the thin tanned leg that's tangled around me. Stealthily, I slide from under her sheets.

God I hope she doesn't wake up. It's never a fun conversation. 'Thanks for last night. It was great. I don't remember your name. No. Don't tell me. I don't really care.' Oh, don't even. Of course I don't remember their names. After a bottle of Jack I barely remember my own.

Stumbling around, I manage to find my boxers and jeans close to her bathroom, and my shirt draped on her dresser.

The process of getting dressed is significantly less fun than the process of getting undressed. Sure, both typically happen in a matter of seconds, but getting naked means I'm about to get off and getting dressed means I'm trying to get out. Completely different types of adrenaline rushing through your system.

Once the only thing I'm missing is my shoes, I feel around my pockets in search of my phone. The search ramps up from casual to panic as I find my keys and wallet, but no phone.

Fuck...I left my phone at home last night. Son of a bitch...Don't look at me like that. If you had the big brother I have you'd leave that shit at home when you're trying to escape too.

I tip toe across the room and grab hers off the nightstand. Thankfully, she doesn't have it password protected.

Major mistake in general. Always keep that shit locked up. You never know what could happen when someone finds it. No, not like me. I don't appreciate that one.

As soon as I sneak out of her room and into the kitchen, I dial my brother's phone number.

It rings twice before he answers, "Speak."

"Middle Man, I need a ride," I mumble into the phone, leaning against a pillar in the kitchen. "Stranded."

"I figured. Your bike's here." He lightly chuckles. "At least you weren't drinking and driving."

"I'm not a complete moron."

What? I'm not.

"Yeah. We'll see. You know Mad Man is pissed."

What else is new? The oldest McCoy brother is always pissed. Always looking for another place to drown all his fucking anger over losing our baby brother just a month ago. He chooses work and riding our asses, I choose liquor and smacking asses. My way is more fun and a little more classic McCoy.

There's a jingle of keys and a deep sigh. "Where are you at?"

"Can't you get Destin to GPS me?"

"He's in the shop," Daniel replies. "You know, the place where you're supposed to be."

I mumble, "Fuck..."

One of the benefits of having a computer genius for a brother is not having to ever actually be lost. Yeah, I know, all phones come with GPS systems, but rarely do they come with the ones that can tell you which routes to avoid because cops are on it when you've just stolen some asshole's 22,000 dollar sculpture for calling you a hood rat. And before you comment, I'm aware that by stealing it I may have proved him right, but by selling it, I became 27,000 dollars richer. Man...that was years ago when stealing still had luster and crime didn't always demand we pay in blood.

"Let me find some mail."

My triplet brother laughs again. "Just like the good old days."

"Shut the fuck up." I move for her kitchen table where there seems to be a magazine opened and other paper products. My search is brief. I'm thankful.

Temporarily stealing her phone and rifling through her shit are not activities I can say I'm enjoying.

"1212 Peach Tree Lane, New Johnsonburg."

"You're in fucking New Johnsonburg," he complains. "You can't fuck chicks closer to home?"

"We both know we've fucked plenty of chicks close to home," I snap. "I'll see you outside in ten."

"It's gonna take me longer than that."

"Fine. Fifteen." I end the call, delete his number, and slide it onto her table under the magazine that clued me into exactly where the hell I am.

If I leave it here, she'll probably assume she did it herself. It won't even register that I might've used it.

Swiftly, I'm out the front door and parked on her sidewalk.

Not quite the walk of shame. More like the Triple D style of avoiding false promises. No matter how up front we are with these chicks in the beginning, most of them still want more from us. From the infamous McCoy brothers. We've been legends since we were in elementary school rocking Power Ranger lunch boxes and tattered hand me down shirts. Then girls wanted to give us their extra cupcakes or cookies just to sit beside them and tell terrible jokes, but as we grew up, chicks offered a lot more than baked treats to try to capture our attention. It probably helps that Madden set up quite the precedence for the McCoy named and gave us tips on how to live up to it. Not just in the bedroom but out of it too.

The sunshine is to the point of blinding, making me further regret having to be up so early. A small pounding tries to creep into my head reminding me why I shouldn't drink so much. Using my hands to rub my temples, I stare at the house across the street where there's a mother trying to feed her baby in a high chair. I stare at the heart warming sight with a dowie smile.

Sometimes I wonder if my mom were still alive just how different life would be. Occasionally I like to think I would've turned out a little more normal. Found some chick to settle down with. Gotten hitched. Had a kid just like that, that she could make a mess trying to feed while I was at work. Sometimes I wonder if my mom were still alive, would we ever have gotten in this fucked up lifestyle?

Daniel pulls up on his motorcycle and immediately offers me a helmet when he stops.

Madden, my oldest brother, is a classic car man. My youngest brother, Merrick, rest his soul, was a sports car kid. The triplets, well, we're all born and bred on bikes. We can ride them all and fix anything that lands in our laps. Daniel prefers crotch rockets. He lives to do stunts when he thinks Madden's not policing him. Destin could go either way, but I like old Harleys. They carry the legend right there in the name. They don't have to mask their greatness behind some French fucking label or fading trend that appeared in the latest car mag.

As soon as I'm settled on the back, he pulls away speedily. I look back to give the house of a future that I'll never have another glance when the front door of my present opens to a frantic leggy blonde.

They're typically blonde. What can I say? I think there's nothing sexier than a blonde head bobbing around on my dick. Oh, like you don't have your favorites?

Daniel flies us from the next town over back to the garage where our apartment is also located. The drive is barely enough time for me to wake up for the long shift that's ahead, but it happens.

More and more frequently since I had to help bury my family twice in month. Our cousin Ben, who was practically Merrick's twin died in a car crash about a week before Merrick was killed...I don't wanna talk about it. Stop bringing it up.

My brother parks his bike on the side beside mine and Destin's. When the three of them are all lined it's like looking at the three of us. They're damn near identical like the three of us. Three black MV Agusta F4CC, easily priced off the line at over a $120,000, each with custom modifications. The seat of each of our bikes has the cursive initial D. Mine has one since I'm the oldest,

Daniel, has two, and Destin three. Other than that, there's no way to distinguish to the outside world which bike belongs to who.

Best part is, we're just the same. All brown eyes. All buzzed cut hair. All toned even if we're thinner than the other McCoys have been. The three of us also have the exact same tatts on our tanned arms and chest, the differences so subtle at first glance you could never tell us apart. Most of the time we're wearing jeans so the extra tatts that don't match don't get seen. But like the bikes, we all pack differences under the hood. I've got a pierced dick. Daniel's got an eyebrow ring he wears occasionally. Destin has an obnoxious as fuck tongue ring. Why the fuck would you wanna pierce your tongue? You have to use that shit daily...and yes, I do use my dick daily, but that's slightly different, don't ya think? I mean what are the chances I'm gonna get a hunk of pizza stuck in the thing?

I put my helmet back on my bike as Daniel sheds the backpack he carried it in. "Bro, Madden's pissed."

Rolling my eyes I sigh, "You said that already."

"Yeah, but like pisssed pissed."

I don't look phased.

"He threw a wrench."

"At least he's not holding all that shit in."

Daniel snickers a little but shakes his head. "Knox is pissed too."

"Shit..."

Knox is basically like having an older sister meets mother figure. Don't get it twisted though. She is just as much one of the McCoys as the rest of us. Fuck, some days I think she's more. The only other person who seems to have that much McCoy pumping through their system is Madden. I really do try to give him as much respect as possible. I get it. It wasn't easy practically raising the four of us, well five if you include Ben. It wasn't like we made that shit easy. Especially us triplets. First week of school every year, the three of us were in the principle's office for some bullshit. Separately we behaved better, but when the three of us were together, which we typically were, shit seemed to always end up with trouble only he could save us from.

"Drew Nathaniel McCoy!" Knoxie's voice pierces my ears.

Fuck. Me. I'm in trouble.

Turning around, I'm not surprised by the irritated expression she's wearing.

Problem with a pissed off Knox isn't just that she looks hot when she's mad, it's that she's violent. Grab me an ice pack?

Her light brown hair blows in the wind. "I'm gonna rip your nut sack off and turn it into a punching bag I use daily in between using your face as one."

Make that two ice packs.

"Good morning to you too, Knox."

"Good?" She stomps her foot at me. "No. Good would've been sleeping in past 7 fucking a.m. Good would've been not having to hustle down the stairs to fill in for some brat who can't even seem to remember that he's not the only fucking person in his house that matters."

On a groan, I complain, "You sound like Madden."

She points a harsh finger at me. "Do. Not. Say. That."

"Then don't act like that," I insist. Knox opens her mouth, but I bite, "Look, you can either spend the next ten minutes chewing me out about my piss poor choices in following my dick over my brain or you can move out of my way, let me change, and get back to the day off you had planned."

Daniel chimes in, "Weren't you supposed to go to the beach or something?"

Confused, I ask, "It's a little cool for a day at the beach, isn't it?"

Knox bites her bottom lip.

Looks like she's got a secret too.

"What do you do at the beach?" Daniel asks.

Sarcastically she snips, "Pick coconuts and pretend I'm Sandie from Sponge Bob."

"I would've never guessed you had a bush like that," Daniel jokes until Knox balls her fist and comes towards him.

She pops him twice in the shoulder and claims, "Two for flinching motherfucker."

"Fuck!" Daniel complains.

I try to stifle my chuckle, which is when she says to me. "Go. Change."

With a nod, I prepare to go, but stop to ask, "We got any more EA? I think I've got like one left."

EA which is the street name for a drug called Enilanerda, is a miracle liquid. Basically it ramps up your immune system to kill any STDs that may try to weasel their way in. One little shot and you don't have to worry about a goddamn thing with one night stands. Hell, for women it also prevents unwanted pregnancies. What the fuck is better than a shot you can take that erases all the problems that comes from fucking around? Yeah, yeah, I know. You're waiting for the catch. Probably why it's not legal. Aside from the money it would cost pharmaceutical companies, no drug is without its drawbacks. EA has an effect on your sex drive. Every time you take it, you run the risk of becoming dependent on it in order to get a hard on or even lose the capability of ever getting one again. Chicks run the same risk as well as being infertile. Sex is a roll of the dice anyway you do it, might as well take the path that suits your lifestyle best.

"Yeah. Vinnie dropped off a delivery this morning. Might I suggest you slow down on putting your dick in anything that's willing to accept it. We don't get free shipments like we used to and while our discount from Vinnie is steep, it's not steep enough."

Playfully I question, "Did you really just ask a McCoy to fuck less?"

She lets out a disgusted groan.

I give her a wink and she slugs me hard in the shoulder as I walk by. Instead of showing her how much that shit stings, I simply laugh and head around the building, using the side door that leaks into the stairwell.

One of the best things about the garage, aside from the expensive beauties that roll in and out for our services, is the fact our apartment is right above it. I love living with my brothers. They're my best friends. Destin, Daniel, and I spend more time with each other than we do anyone else. We've been that way since we were kids, never figured out a good reason to stop living life that way.

Inside I stroll passed the kitchen and to the right down the hallway. At the split, I turn the direction of my room. I pass Daniel's, the bathroom we share, and head right for my room that is in the same condition I left it.

Is it wrong part of me hopes Knoxie will go all mother hen just once and clean it for me? Hey, she cleans Madden's room for him. A dude can dream.

Tossing off my clothes that wreak of booze, cigarettes, and expensive perfume, I fumble around the piles of clothes that need to be folded or washed.

I know it's sad that the two once separate piles have now morphed into one booby trap. At least it protects my door from unwanted guests.

I grab a pair of work pants and one of my white shirts that has my name embroidered over the pocket. As soon as my shoes are on, I look around the room for my cell phone.

There's no telling where that shit is.

Carelessly, I knock the car mags off my night stand, rifle through my top drawer past the empty vials I know I need to toss. Thankful I have one left that's full, I grab it, and a fresh needle.

Between the piercings and tattoos I have, needles don't even cause an eyebrow raise any more. You might wanna look the other way if you're squeamish. Don't worry. It's only gonna take a second.

Once I'm done, I toss the empty vile back in the drawer and the needle in the disposal container that's specifically for them.

Before you start questioning why I have one of those but can't throw the vial away, Knox bought us those years ago to use and two...I'm lazy. Whatever.

I return to searching for my phone. Feeling a little annoyed at the fact I can't find the damn thing, I growl as I hunt under my bed around half empty soda bottles and energy drinks.

"You know it might help if you clean your fucking room," Madden's voice pulls me up to my feet.

Madden is scary as fuck. Triple D, which is what we've been nick named since we came home from the hospital, we're intimidating only when we need to be. Madden's face is sharp with nothing soft to it. The jagged scar along his jaw bone line doesn't help the stone cold killer look he portrays. Before you ask if he is or isn't, let me ask you something. Would you blame him if he was because it was the only way he knew to protect this family? To make sure we weren't killed instead? It's fucked up, but we live in a kill or be killed lifestyle. And now that the youngest two of the crew are dead, his kill instinct has jumped. Severely.

"Yeah, but then I wouldn't have a good excuse for being late to work."

"You never have a good fucking excuse."

I shrug before I toss my pillows around finding it resting underneath.

Bastard...Sleeping in my bed without me.

"Where the fuck were you last night?"

"You want her name or address?" My sarcasm causes his jaw to tick.

He's not in the mood for my bullshit, but if we're talking about not being in the mood, I'm not in it for his. A little hungover here.

Madden folds his arms across his chest. "That shit's not funny Triple D."

"Nothing's funny to you any more, Mad Man." With a shake of my head I slide my phone in my back pocket. "You're not the only one who lost family. You're not the only one who lost a fucking brother. With all due respect, we're all entitled to cope, even if it's not the same way you do."

He doesn't hesitate to call me out on my bullshit. "You call putting back a bottle a night and fucking chicks like you're in the Slut Olympics, coping?"

"Better than riding my brothers into the ground with work while turning my dick into a rusted tool," I counter.

I expect him to break down and yell. Jump down my throat and scream until I listen yet he simply says, "Do whatever the fuck you need to do to deal with this shit, but stop leaving your fucking phone at home." My mouth twitches to open and he continues, "The shit with The Devil isn't over. I'm not prepared to lose another fucking brother because he couldn't get his dick scratched at home where I knew he was fucking safe, so I'm gonna tell you one last fucking time. Come. Home. At. Night."

"Seriously?" I snap. "You don't get to dictate that shit! It might have worked with Merrick-"

He points a finger at me. "Don't."

My mouth shuts.

Fuck. Did I forget to mention he's basically put a ban on using our dead baby brother's name? And our cousin's? I don't fucking know if he thinks it's gonna make the pain of them being gone hurt any more than it already does or what. I hate to be the one to break it to him. It can't possibly hurt any more than it already does.

"Madden," Knox's voice comes from over his shoulder.

Both of our attention turns to her.

"We've um...we've got a situation downstairs." The expression on her face lets me know it's one that should have us all worried.

Knox isn't your run of the mill chick. She's a McCoy. Not much scares or worries her, us aside. She has a pair of nuts as strong as the rest of us for the bullshit we endure, so if she looks scared there's a damn fucking good reason.

Madden quickly moves past her with me right behind him. The moment we hit the shop on the bottom floor, it's obvious what has Knox rattled.

"Oh look, the cheerleader ran to get the captain of this piece of shit shop," one of the police officers says, pulling his sunglasses off his face.

Fucking cops. So many are crooked there's very little reason to believe any exist to actually protect and serve the community.

Madden folds his arms across his chest once more. This time, I follow the action and stand beside him.

I'm the second oldest. I'm the one shit falls on when it rolls off of Madden. Believe it or not I'm the most responsible of Triple D.

Unimpressed by their presence, I ask, "Can we help you?"

The other cop, who reminds me of Seth Rogen with less of the charm, starts to point. "Everything in this shop legal?"

Without waiting for Madden to speak I announce, "We run a legit business."

Sunglasses leans against the wall. "Can you prove that?"

Destin speaks, "Every day that ends in y."

"And all these parts?" Sunglasses chomps on his gum. "These are 'legit' too?"

"Every. Single. One." I assure. "Now, is there a service you were looking for?"

"Watch your tone," the Seth Rogen look alike snaps. "You're speaking to an officer of the law."

"No he's not," Daniel mouths off from under the hood of a Ferrari.

Yeah. That's Daniel. Iron balls and brainless.

Stepping to the side he wipes the grease off his hands with a rag. "He's talking to a puppet of The Devil."

Sunglasses nods. "One puppet would recognize another."

"We don't do shit for The Devil anymore," Madden speaks for the first time. "And just so we're all on the same fucking page, you can give him a message, I'm coming for him...."

"You sound a little bitter McCoy," the curly hair cop says sliding his hands in his pocket. "Hell, if I didn't know any better I'd say you were pissed like it was you who was being watched by IA."

So the truth comes to light. They're pissed off because instead of gliding under the radar like all of The Devil's cops always have, they're being watched.

"Someone sold out a bunch of us to IA," Sunglasses growls. "We've got reason to believe it was a McCoy."

"We don't really like red and blues," Daniel's sneer makes me and Destin chuckle.

"Obviously," I add.

"So why would we walk into a place surrounded by them to snitch out you rats?" Daniel says joining my side. "That doesn't sound very bright."

Destin moves so he's standing next to Daniel. "That doesn't sound very safe."

A McCoy wall. It rarely happens and when it does it's never a good thing. Hell, kind of like having all of us in the same room outside of a party. It usually means something bad is about to come.

"Well someone is selling out names that only you fuckers could have," curly hair growls. "And we don't appreciate it."

"Thems the breaks," Daniel smugly replies.

Curly head makes a motion for my brother, "You smart mouth fuck up I swear-"

"One hand." I interrupt immediately. "One hand on my brother and I'll drop you where you stand."

He stops. "Did you just threaten a cop?"

Casually I look around Madden at Knox. "Would you call that a threat, Knox?"

"More like a promise," she corrects.

"A guar-an-fucking-tee," Daniel backs me.

Like the punk bitch he is, the cop shuts his mouth.

Sunglasses surrenders his hands. "Before we leave, we just wanna express our condolences, Madden." The words twitch his fist as much as they do mine. "I mean, it's gotta be tough to keep burying McCoys six feet under."

"Either make an arrest or get the fuck out," Destin growls.

Pleased, by the reaction Sunglasses puts them back on his face. "Keep your head up and eyes open McCoys. The Devil's not done with you yet."

At that he uses his arm to brush the shelf beside him knocking tools, paperwork, and oils to the ground. Instantly I twitch to lunge forward when Madden places a hand on my bicep to stop me.

With a chuckle Sunglasses backs up slowly. "Oops."

The Seth Rogen doppelganger follows in the dickhead's footsteps by smashing in the tail light of the Ferrari Daniel was working on. "Whoopsie."

We watch as the two of them head away from the building chuckling to themselves. Once they've pulled away in their cop car, Daniel shouts, "Fuck!" He tosses his arms in the air. "That's gonna fucking cost us! Time and money!"

Knox sighs, "I'll cancel my plans for the day and suit up. I can handle that while you focus on what's under the hood."

"But it's your day off," Daniel points out. "Didn't you have waves to eat or sun to slurp up."

"Ugh," she mumbles. "Shut up."

He rolls his eyes and walks away towards the car that was damaged, still cussing under his breath. Destin strolls off back towards the office, most likely to call the owner about the unexpected damage.

Computer genius and the best customer service manners out of all of us. I'm not worried about him finding a nice way to lie about what happened.

Knox turns to head upstairs but not before Madden gives her a nod of appreciation for her sacrifice. She accepts that as being enough and exits, leaving us standing alone.

He quietly growls, *"That's* why I want you to come home at night." His eyes lower to me. "Do you get it now?"

I don't answer.

"This is fucking war, Triple D. This shit doesn't stop until someone at the top of the pyramid is dead. I'd rather it be him than me," he states coldly. "Are we fucking clear?"

Without a word spoken, I nod.

He grunts and storms away to clean up the mess that was created by Sunglasses.

My life has become a war zone. Saddest thing is....we're losing. We're losing left and right. We used to work for The Devil, a king pen with his hands in so many pockets, you'd have a better chance at hitting one of those jackpots in Vegas for millions of dollars than the likeliness of him being caught. We used to move cars, money, and drugs mainly. Occasionally weapons. Not dealers, just movers. Getting that shit from one place to another in a quick fashion. Without us, he's suffering moving the weight he used to and without him we're no longer bringing in millions. More importantly, we're no longer the complete family we once were. For that he'll have to pay the only way that's right. With his fucking life.

Drew

"I will see your blonde little minx from last night, raise you two, and add on the Thursday morning usual, forty two minutes after they left." Daniel points his glass at me. "Now *that's* the McCoy way."

Shaking my head, I laugh. "Middle Man, your dick's gonna fall off."

"I always EA bro," he assures.

"From excessive use."

"Hey, my dick needs to nut up or shut up, ya feel me?" Daniel laughs and shoots back the last of his drink. "I am the master of this dick."

"Yeah, yell that a little louder and watch girls flock," Destin sighs now shaking his head. "Seriously, can you hear yourself?"

"He's in fucking surround sound," I comment, pushing my glass away from me. "How can he not hear himself?"

Destin follows my action. "How do we not get kicked out of this place?"

"Mickey's is home away from home," Daniel asserts. Slamming his empty glass down he states loudly, "And Mickey's loves fucking McCoys!"

Azura, the usual bartender appears in front of us, the bottle of SoCo already in her possession. "Who doesn't love the McCoys?"

"Exactly!" Daniel agrees.

She giggles at his over enthusiastic body movements.

He put back four shots when we got here before we started downing mixed drinks. Apparently the shit that went down with the crooked cops hit him a little harder than he wanted to admit out loud. That's the thing with Middle Man. He doesn't like to talk about shit. He'd rather drink away the pain and then return to having a good time. Like just enough liquor completely washes away whatever pissed him off and fun Triple D returns. He's kind of simple. And yeah...I know. It's kind of sad.

I watch the slightly nerdy mocha colored woman fill my glass. Feeling a little feisty myself, I challenge, "Can you even tell the difference between us?"

"Of course."

"You do know we're identical, right?" Destin adds as she fills the rest of my glass with Sprite.

Don't judge. I'm looking to get just enough buzz to make it back home with something soft and easy under my arm, not forget where I am. Madden's right. I need to bring my ass home no matter how much I hate being there because it's so fucking obvious what's missing.

"Like on paper. Like doctors thought we were photocopied in the womb type of shit," Destin continues.

We're all in jeans and black t-shirts tonight too. That wasn't on purpose. It's all I had that was clean. Now in school...that was a different story. Daniel and I may or may not have had Destin let down clingy girls nicely for us. Yeah. I told you. We were trouble. Don't try correct me. I'm less trouble now thank you very much.

Azura fills his glass up next, her glasses slightly falling down her nose. When she's finished she looks up and points to me. "Drew. His voice is slightly lower than both of yours. He also rarely wide smiles to where he shows all his teeth. My guess is because of the chipped tooth towards the back you can only see when he really laughs."

Chipped it on my first motorcycle ride. It's just a little piece. Most people never notice.

"Daniel." She points to the other end. "Has an eyebrow ring. He's also left handed and tends to lean to the side no matter what he's doing." Without breaking eye contact, she finishes with, "And you...Destin...have toffee colored eyes. When you smile, it's always crooked. More hidden and softer than your brothers. You also have a tongue ring."

You get the feeling she knows us a little too well for comfort?

"You McCoys think no one can tell you apart, but the truth is no matter how well you blend together at first glance, you're very different." She finally breaks eye contact from Destin and looks at Daniel. "You want some Captain?"

"You know me so well."

She smirks and turns to grab the bottle.

"However, I am not left handed."

I lean forward to look down at him. "Yes you are motherfucker. Do you know how hard that shit was to learn?"

Pretending to be Daniel is definitely the most complicated.

"I'm good with both my hands." He makes jerk off motions with each of them until Destin and I erupt into laughter.

Destin mumbles, "You're a fucking moron..."

"Yeah, yeah," he brushes him as Azura fills up his glass. "Big talk coming from someone who pierced their tongue. *That* was some moronic shit."

Destin rolls the jewelry around. "At least mine serves a purpose."

"To add unnecessary sound effects to you eating a sandwich?" I joke lifting my glass. "I'm pretty we could do without that bullshit."

Destin lifts his eyebrows. "A tongue ring in the bedroom is self-explanatory, such is a cock ring-"

"Guilty."

"Also moronic." Daniel points at me. "Who willingly lets someone put a needle like that near their dick?"

Quickly I argue, "Who lets someone put one that close to their fucking eye?"

"I'd rather lose an eye than paralyze my cock." He gives us an over exaggerate shudder. "In fact, excuse me while I go insure it still works."

Destin and I raise our glasses at him as he wanders off.

"He's an idiot," Destin sighs before having a sip of his drink.

"Definitely."

There's only a brief pause before Daniel yells, "Triple D, get your asses over here!"

I could've told you that was coming.

Turning around, I spot him posted up at a table with three blondes, his arm already draped around one.

It's how he calls dibs without having to say it.

"That was quick," Destin mumbles following me over.

"Oh my God," one of the other girls squeaks. "It's really you! It's really Triple D!"

Daniel wiggles his eyebrows. "Live in the flesh baby."

My body parks next to the one who's biting her bottom lip, a slightly inebriated glaze already in her green eyes.

A walk in the park. All it takes is the McCoy name to make panties drop.

"Drew McCoy," I announce.

"Candice," she coos back. With a giggle she leans towards me, the shot of her tits now perfect. "Is it true what they say about McCoys?"

See.

I wet my lips. "Depends."

"On?"

"On what you're asking." Having a small sip of my drink I reply, "Because you better fucking believe we finish first in the streets and last in the sheets."

Excited, she lifts her eyebrows. "Buy me a drink?"

I offer her mine. "Take this one."

"What is it?"

"Already bought."

She smiles and has a sip.

Do I enjoy being a dick? Fine. You caught me. Sometimes. But the other thing that comes with the McCoy name is the expected McCoy attitude. Apparently chicks dig dick in the bed and out. Is it always fun to live up to what the world expects you to be? What do you think?

For another hour or so, the two other girls put back shots trying to keep up with Daniel who could give a professional frat boy a run for their money. It's clear that the girl who should've been for Destin is going to go home with Daniel. At least at first.

Wouldn't be surprised if she ended up sneaking down the hall to Destin's room when she was done. Shit happens more often than you would imagine. They try one D they wanna try the others.

Luckily for me, Candice has been all over me, desperate to keep my attention off her sorority sisters who seem to be anxious to get back to our apartment. Just as her hand slides across my crotch for the fifth time, she sighs, "I would love to take a ride with you...."

"With me or on me babe?"

Her eyes light up. "Both."

Nodding slowly, I stand. "Let me close the tab and grab a smoke."

"Be quick," she tries to command.

I lift my eyebrows. "You'll wait as long you have to."

She wiggles in her seat, obviously enjoying being talked to like that.

Wow. Fucking, really? That's a little pathetic right? That she gets off being talked to like she's less of a person? Fuck...it's pathetic I enjoy doing it.

At the bar, I pull out my wallet. "Hey Azura, what do I owe you?"

Azura punches a few buttons on the machine closer to the liquor. "For just you or the whole Triple D crew?'

"All of us."

"135."

A whistle comes out of me. "Damn."

"That's with a discount," she informs, printing out my receipt. When it lands in front of me she states, "You McCoys really do go big or go home."

"No," I deny, tossing twenties on top of it. "We go big and then go home. There's no or." Stuffing my wallet back in my back pocket I tell her, "Keep it all. Tips in there."

She picks up the stack. "Thanks Drew."

Casually I toss her a wave and head outside to the front of the building for a quick smoke.

Not exactly a habit I'm proud of. Picked it up when I started putting back enough liquor to drive a bar out of business. Madden doesn't know and I'd like to keep it that way. He thinks smoking makes you weak. Then again he thinks a lot of things make you weak. My point is, I don't need to give him anything else to be pissed off at me about. Sure, I deserve some of it, but let's not add to the list. And just so we're clear, I'm not scared of my oldest brother or some sick shit like that. I respect him, even when I don't agree with him. Anyone who gives up their entire life to protect someone else's gets major credit in my book, but someone who gives up their entire life to protect their entire family because their parents are dead, that person is a fucking hero.

Lighting the cigarette on the deserted corner, I stare out at the highway, the constant passing headlights and humming of engines, a gear heads' lullaby. I blow out smoke while getting lost in the memories that come from the simple sight.

I swear it was just yesterday we were doing basic stunts on these streets. Racing up and down that highway. Racing for respect. Racing for chicks. Then it was cash. Making the McCoy name one asshole left in the exhaust at time. Back then running from the cops meant something completely different.

Suddenly there's a pair of footsteps coming from behind me. I turn around assuming I'll see a defeated Destin when I'm shocked by the sight of the dude in a black ski mask. Instinctively, my fist balls, preparing to swing when another sound of footsteps rushes at me from the other side. In one swift motion I'm attacked from both sides, my cigarette hitting the sidewalk in the scuffle. My fists swing, landing in the jaw of one, then the gut of the other. One hits back, the blow landing in my kidney, doubling me over as the other one brings his knee up to my chin, making my teeth click. Growling through the pain I straighten back up, my elbow nailing one in the nuts. He drops, giving me a chance to stumble away quickly for help, my stride is cut short. A burning sensation shoots through my leg dropping me to the ground. I do my best to keep crawling forward, knowing if I make it to the window someone will see. Someone will help me.

Help! Go! Call someone! Yell at them for me! Do something!

Unfortunately, another masked figure appears in front of me and places a moist cloth over my face. With my final breath, the sharp scent attaches itself to my system, shutting it down effortlessly.

Melody

"But I don't understand," Omar scratches his bald, tan head. "How can any plant do that?"

"Plants are remarkable," I hum turning the page in my botany book.

They are. They're so underrated. Sometimes I feel I'm just like them. Mistaken for something weak and disposable. I know that's how The Devil views me. That's how he views everyone.

There's a commotion among the voices outside the plane that lifts my attention off my book.

"You weren't supposed to fucking shoot him, Rex!" JJ, one of The Devil's flunkies, gripes to another. "If he's dead, we're dead!"

"It was a leg shot!' Rex argues as they drag a limp body onto the plane. "He ran! What did you want me to do?"

"You two would've been fucked without me," Lamar, another member of the Three Stooges adds.

That's what I call them when they're together. Not quite as funny as the show, but definitely dumber at times. I know what you're thinking. It's not possible. I've come to realize, most things people think are impossible, are what I'm most likely to encounter. Hell, how do you think I got here?

"We're fucked with you!" JJ shouts.

"He's lost a lot of blood," Rex sighs. They drop the body at my feet like puppies would a bone. "At least I think he has. If anyone can fix him Melody can. Melody is amazing."

Concerned I ask, "What do you mean fix him?" When they don't reply I snap, "You were supposed to put the rag over his face and bring him aboard. Two simple steps. The rag would do the heavy work-"

"Lifting that asshole is heavy," Lamar whines.

"Oh please," JJ grumbles. "You barely lifted his feet."

"You barely lifted his feet!"

"That doesn't make any sense!"

"Shut up," Omar commands.

Knowing their place in the pecking order they immediately do as they're told. The three of them gather around with their heads hung. Omar moves to stand beside me, but doesn't comment.

His jeans seems to be rubricating. "He's bleeding."

"I uh..." Rex looks up. "I might've shot him."

Omar growls, "Why would you shoot him?"

"He was running away," Rex quickly tries to explain. "I had to stop him! He couldn't get back to the bar! If we-"

"Shut up and get me the iron." Dropping to my knees, I state, "JJ get me my med kit."

"We need to be in the air," Omar whispers out. In a harsh movement he pushes the squad out of the way to head for the pilot. "The Devil wants us in the air!"

Working for a man who could probably make actual angels cry is awful. I didn't sign up for this and every chance he gets he reminds me of it. If it wasn't for Omar, I probably would've overdosed myself out of this shit by now.

"Rex give me your belt," I demand.

The body that was still just seconds ago starts a low groan as his head moves back and forth.

"Really?" My face darts up. "I thought you said you drugged him."

"I put the rag over his face," Lamar insists, bringing me the iron. "I swear!"

I snatch it from him. With a pinned look I ask, "Which rag, Lamar?"

"The white one."

"The white one was the test rag!"

"Why did you need a test rag?" He yells back.

"Because it wasn't the only solution I needed to mix and you morons are always messing with my shit before it's labeled!" Frustrated, I toss my hands in the air. "Fucking unbelievable..."

JJ drops my med kit next to my feet just as I plug in the iron. "What happened?"

"Wrong rag," Rex mumbles. "And I'm an idiot cause I shot him."

"You didn't have to fucking shoot him," the arguing starts again with Lamar.

"At least I stopped him," he fights. "Better than half ass knocking him out."

There's another heavy groan and the body moves. Knowing I need to act fast, I grab my scissors and cut his pant leg exposing the wound. Quickly I disinfect it, more grunts of discomfort rolling out of him.

"Good news, Rex," I sigh. "You're a terrible fucking shot."

"I pinned him in the leg!"

"You grazed his leg." The correction causes his partners in crime to snicker.

Thankfully. Thankfully it grazed his leg. I hate pulling out bullets almost as much as I hate what I'm about to do next.

Carefully I wrap the belt around his exposed leg to help stop the blood flow before grabbing the heated iron to cauterize the wound. The second the heat hits his skin, he arches up, a cry of agony so fierce coming out of him, my heart darts into my throat.

That's...that's never happened before. No. Not the screaming thing. That always happens. Have you ever been burned before? Exactly. I meant the heart thing. I've never hurt for someone like him before. That's not good. Neither is the extra step I was required to add to this process.

"Fuck..." he grumbles, his eyes still struggling to open.

In a flawless motion, I wrap the freshly closed area with a bandage from my med kit. "It's alright," I try to comfort him quietly. "It's gonna be alright..."

"Burn a motherfucker with an iron then lies to him about it being alright.." JJ mutters. "And they call us heartless."

"Shut up and get my bag from by the window," I whisper as my hand reaches up to touch his flushed face.

How can anyone still look beautiful when they're cringing in this much pain?

With a gentle stroke I reassure him, "The pain will fade."

"Promise?"

Hearing his voice so weak and helpless causes me to respond immediately, "Promise."

Once my bag is in my hands, I pull out the mixture and a fresh rag.

You've seen how stupid these guys are. Of course I keep spare everything. Wouldn't you?

I dampen the rag and place it over his face. "Now breathe..."

He takes one large inhale and drifts off the way he should've originally. At the sight of him knocked out once more, part of me feels at ease.

At least he's not in pain at this very minute. With what's ahead of him at least he'll have this. It's more than most get.

Omar points. "You three, front of the plane, now." The three of them sulk the direction they were instructed. When it's just the two of us he shakes his head. "Don't look at him like that."

Instead of denying anything, I shift my attention to cleaning my hands of the knock out mixture. "Like what?"

"Like you did, Jimmy."

Just hearing his name causes my body to tense. "I don't know what you're talking about."

"You know exactly what I'm talking about, Melody. You were stupid once and managed to live. Be stupid twice and you'll for sure die," he harshly states.

Omar doesn't say anything else before he turns around to stalk off the way he came.

He's right. I know he's right. The problem isn't knowing he's right. It's knowing that what I'm doing is wrong and having to do it anyway. Welcome to Hell. I'm not a visitor. I'm an employee.

Drew

Angels, aren't real right? And if they were, which I am not saying they are, shouldn't they be blonde? We already talked about my blonde obsession. Honestly, I think it's because my mom was a brunette. She was the most gorgeous woman in the entire world. Just the most stunning in beauty and personality. She was also the most supportive and fucking lovable person I could think of. She is what truly made a McCoy boy into a man, so I think that's how I view brunettes. They should be treated with respect. They should be kept as the one woman you wanna keep forever. I've never met a woman who I ever considered keeping. Never figured I would. Until now. You didn't answer my question. Are angels real?

The brunette woman adjusts her long braid. "You're awake."

"Are you the Angel of Death?" I groan through the throbbing pain in my head. "Am I in Heaven?"

"Hell."

So I'm not always the smartest guy and I may not know as much about lore as other people, but I'm pretty sure angels are a Heaven thing right?

My eyes struggle to focus, but when they do, the sight in front of me makes me want to question her again about her angel status. Her olive skin looks soft enough to blanket more than just the pain in my body away. The long braid she seems to be fiddling with would wrap nicely around my hand while those brown eyes that are sparkling at me would look even sweeter, brighter from the orgasm I'd give her.

No, I'm not ignoring her perfectly curved figure that's trying to hide under those white scrubs. I'm just trying to be a gentleman and not mention it. So what if I just mentioned giving her an orgasm? What's your point?

"Stop looking at me like that," she sharply whispers.

With a crooked smile I ask, "Like what?"

"Like I'm every other girl that's ever crossed the McCoy path."

"You're so far from it..."

She tries to hide her smirk, but I see it.

You see it too, don't you? I told you. McCoys are hard to resist.

Groaning once more, I drag my body upward and lean it against the pillows behind me. "Where am I?"

"You're in one of my many homes," a voice I recognize says from somewhere in the background. Melody steps to the side and reveals a face on the screen I was hoping the next time I saw it would be in a news report about being found dead. "Welcome."

No, he's not here for his Forbes magazine photo shoot. He is one of the most wanted criminals in the country. I can easily see how you think those two things could go hand in hand, but this time they don't. Well, is there a criminal edition of that mag?

I rub the back of my neck. "Your hospitality has been generous."

"You're alive, aren't you?"

Don't agree with him.

"For a purpose." My reply makes him smirk. "What the fuck do you want?"

"Right to the point. You have learned a thing or two from the oldest of you McCoys." He leans back in his office chair. "You're here to do a job for me."

"Fuck you," I bite. "We don't fucking work for you anymore. That's what happens when you kill our fucking family."

He nods and snaps his fingers. At that moment the screen splits in half revealing Daniel, tied up in a chair, slightly bruised, with duct tape on his mouth and gun against the back of his head.

Shit...

"I have no problem killing more of you if necessary," he states. "I only need two of you triplets for this job and as far as I'm concerned one less McCoy is never a bad thing. Now, would you like to watch your brother's brains paint my basement wall or shall I continue?"

I swear I can feel the pressure of that loaded weapon against the back of my own head.

With a deep growl I shake my head. "What do you want?"

He waves his hand and the weapon lowers from Daniel's skull. His camera angle expands wide across the screen, but in the corner the view of Middle Man remains.

Worse conference call ever.

"There are two things that are missing from my life because of you fucking McCoys."

I try not to smirk. "We didn't blow up your house."

He glares. "The only reason I believe that is because your brother burned in the flames." Hearing the words forces my face down and The Devil takes the exposed weakness like a bone being tossed to a full pup. "Oh no...sensitive subject? You don't wanna discuss how your baby brother barely had time to say a final prayer before he was screaming in torment?"

The image of my twenty three year old brother losing his life like that churns my stomach.

Thanks for your apologies.

Clearly pleased, he smiles. "My compound, which has all been burned to the ground at this point, was not what I was referring to. Due to McCoys being hell bent on revenge, my inside men on the force are dropping like flies. I. Do. Not. Like. This."

Shaking my head I deny, "Like we told your punk ass flunkies that fucked up our shop. We're coming for you, but it won't be like that. Narking on you like that isn't our style."

"Regardless." His hand waves in the air. "Whoever is knocking out my players in the system is costing me a fortune *and* preventing me from acquiring things I've had planned to be in my possession for months. Show them."

The woman in white presents a tablet in front of me with a photo of two different objects. One is sculpture of some kind and the other...the other is artwork on two wheels.

"By your expression, you are well aware of what that is."

"That's The Phantom Black Princess."

"The 1934 BMW R7x," he announces. "Price unknown because in theory it doesn't exist."

"It doesn't."

"The most valuable things do not exist on paper, Drew."

The 1934 BMW R7 is really a motorcycle, if you must call it that. It's one of the most beautiful crafted pieces of machinery to ever exist. It had disappeared until a few years ago when it was discovered and restored to it's original condition. Literally art on wheels. Many of the designs were inspired by Art Deco. There was a prototype made, which was declared, would be too expensive to mass produce. The project was shelved. The BMW R7x is a rumor that the designer who had a special place for his shelved project, started another in his free time. One just slightly better. One with just a little extra edge. Hints the x. It's just a ghost story. A useless legend told at old biker bars. Uncle D used to tell it to us when he'd tuck us in at night. Ben, his son, used to promise he'd find that bike one day.

"This was supposed to be ceased at a raid and brought to me," The Devil explains his eyebrows now furrowed. "But due to many of my allies in the legal system disappearing, the raid was put on hold before being thrown out altogether. This bike should already be in my possession."

Still in disbelief I shake my head. "That's not real."

"It is 100 percent real. I've seen the beauty in person. She's been appraised and authenticated. They don't want it in the news or on paper. A lost secret. Fine." He surrenders his hands. "I don't give a shit. I have a buyer for it."

"The statue too?"

"That's for me. A little feel better present for all the pain and distress you McCoys have been putting me through."

My eyes cut back to the art piece.

I don't know that much shit about art. That was Merrick's department. He was always spouting off facts and rambling about famous artists. This just looks like a misshapen claw to me.

"The statue, like the bike, has a value with enough zeros to make me a forgiving man." When my eyes look back up he says, "Now, Daniel you will be in charge of making me a mock bike, as well as ones for you to use for your transportation. While Drew, you will be in charge of not only making me a mock statue but the false prints and facial pieces you will be needing to complete this task."

Annoyed, I shake my head again.

Can't fucking believe this...

"Melody has a picture of the statue as well as the man, the two of you will be impersonating. He's a prince."

"Y-y-y-you're having us pretend to be royalty?"

"Yes. So brush up your manners," The Devil instructs.

I take a deep breath in an attempt to regain my composure. "How'd this prince get on your bad side?"

"That's none of your concern," he snaps. "Like Madden, you need to learn your place. In this kingdom, I am the lion. I will take what I want when I want it and you...and your brothers are all like little lionesses, just waiting to grovel and eat my scraps."

Did he...did he just call us his bitches? Swallowing that bullet sounds much better than working another day for this fucker.

"Speaking of Madden, before you do that thing you McCoys are well known for, he's...unavailable at this time to lend his assistance."

Nervous of the possibilities of how he's torturing my big brother I clench my fists together. "What the fuck does that mean?"

"That means, him and Destin are battling a little thing called an audit. Doesn't sound like such a big deal, but I think you've forgotten how your money in the beginning for that shop got bankrolled."

I wet my lips, but remain silent.

Please tell me you hate him as much as the rest of us by now. Good news is Destin has those tracks covered on paper and digitally to the point that besides an inside man's confession you couldn't ever figure it out. Our money is laundered, put away in bank accounts including Swiss ones, so the search is useless, other than to keep my brothers occupied.

Realizing I have no choice, I shrug. "What's the plan?"

"That will be revealed to the two of you on a later date. As for now, *you* have thirteen days to create your identities and my statue, which you eyeballed like it would be easy."

I've done a forgery once or seven times in my life. They don't have to be perfect. Just fucking believable.

"But again...you McCoys need an attitude adjustment." The corner of his mouth lifts. "Consider this it."

The screen goes black not giving me another chance to say a word to him or my brother.

Immediately I snap my head at the woman. "Bring him back!"

"I can't."

"Yes, you fucking can!" I shout. "Bring him back! I wanna make sure my brother is okay!"

"He's fine," she softly answers.

"How the fuck do you know?"

"Because I know where he is. Nina will tend to his wounds. Levi will not lay another hand on him unless necessary." She motions a hand to the door way where there's a large tan bald man with his arms folded. "Much like Omar."

Omar looks like a Hispanic Mike Tyson without the tattoos.

"And who are you?"

"Melody." She tries to offer me a smile of comfort that I brush off with an eye roll. "You will need-"

"Why aren't we together?" I cut her off, pushing on her patience by the way she sighs. "Why is Daniel there and I'm here?"

"Would you want two McCoys conspiring together in the same house?"

Good point.

"Besides, Daniel is in charge of a timely and crucial mock rebuild along with two custom jobs to make this possible. He is where he needs to be. A place where parts are easily accessible at any given time of day or night, along with assistance from Nina, who can handle the help if he requires it."

"And me?"

"You're where you need to be. I will be responsible for gathering your supplies as well as the herbs you will be burying in the hollow statue." Before I can question anything else she points to the tablet. "Please list the items you will need. Any and all. Additional trips can be made, but please try to be as thorough as possible this time."

Running away doesn't seem like a good call, but getting a message to the outside world seems possible if I can get out of this room.

"I wanna go with you."

She folds her hands behind her back. "It's not a possibility."

"Then I won't make the list."

Omar pulls the gun from his holster and points it.

"Then Omar will be forced to end your life and your brothers will not get the chance to bury you." The tone in her voice sounds pleading. "Please, make the list."

I nod.

I don't have any fucking moves to make. Not a single one. The Devil wins again.

Melody

Bringing the grocery bags into the kitchen of the only place I've really called home in years, I drop them onto the counters trying to drown out the lecture Omar has been spewing since we pulled into the driveway.

"Melody-"

"I heard you," I snap over my shoulder. "And I heard you yesterday when you said it. And on the plane. But I don't agree with you."

"But you can't see you the way I can."

Ceasing all movements, I turn around to face him. "Omar, I appreciate you. I appreciate all you've done for me over the years. You're the closest thing I've got to family any more, but you have to know, I know what I'm doing. I'm a professional. I will do my job."

He looks unconvinced.

When I first got stranded in this world, Omar went out of his way to shelter me from things. After a few months I learned it was because he lost custody of his daughter early on in life because his wife didn't approve of his lifestyle. He always said it was probably for the best his little girl didn't have to live in a world like this, but I think the guilt still ate at him until I arrived. It was like getting a second chance. For both of us. My father wasn't in my life either. Overdose.

I plead, "A little trust please."

"In this job? Never."

The sound of a door opening, grabs both of our attention. Our eyes dart across the living room of the small cottage to where Drew is opening his white bedroom door with a heavy yawn.

Is this place the most beautiful? No, but I've tried to make it as homey as possible. The interior is white walls and dark wood floors while the décor is a combination of beach themed and country living. Sounds a little strange, but look around. It flows pretty well.

Drew's boxers are barely hanging on his slender hips and his tight chest is completely exposed courtesy of the shirt idea he apparently abandoned. The muscles masked underneath the colorful tattoos has my bottom lip jumping between my teeth.

Do not ask me the last time I saw a man naked who wasn't being tortured.

Omar clears his throat.

Busted.

Omar growls, "You don't feel you have to wear clothes?"

Drew grunts and shrugs, eyes now on me. "Do you blame me?"

Was he flirting? I know. I know. He's a McCoy. They flirt with anything that can breathe on it's own, but....Damn it. Omar's right. I may have trouble staying focused. You'll help me, right?

"Besides, you or one of the goons who jumped me took my clothes to search them for weapons."

"How do you know that's what they were taken for?" Omar stands at attention, eyes cutting me a glance. "Who told you that?"

Drew's confusion is immediate. "No one."

"Then how do you know that?"

"'Cause I'm not a moron. You didn't take then to get them dry cleaned, so to make sure I wasn't packing was the next logical conclusion." Omar's shoulders slightly relax. "Now, can I get one of my smokes?"

"You have spare clothes in the drawers of your room. A fresh pack of cigarettes has been placed in there as well," I calmly answer.

He gives Omar one more harsh look before he retreats to change. The moment the door shuts Omar whispers, "I hate McCoys."

A small grin comes to my face as I return to unpacking the groceries. "Why? Because they're funny?"

"Because they're like parasites. Hard to exterminate," Omar answers before he starts to place the bags containing the requested work materials on the round kitchen table.

"To one side please. We have to have room to eat."

"He can eat on the floor like the fungus he is."

I roll my eyes. "Stop being dramatic."

"I'm not," he insists before his cell phone thankfully rings. There's a short pause before he states, "I have to go. I'll be back to pick you up at two."

Once I'm alone in the kitchen, I finally let out a breath.

Don't get me wrong. Omar is the closest thing to family I have in this world, but I'm not dumb enough to believe for one moment his loyalty lies anywhere near me when The Devil's best interests are on the table. Loyalty to The Devil comes first. It's that or die. Facts are facts.

"Is he always so friendly?" Drew's voice appears closer than I expect.

Quickly, I turn around to see him just a couple feet from me, a cigarette dangling from his fingertips, his bottom half now in sweat pants with no underwear and still very shirtless.

Very, very shirtless. Could I be his shirt? Oh God. I'm gonna get myself killed thinking like that. Okay, so....you think it for me...Deal?

My answer is said on a chuckle. "Yes."

Drew offers me a smile. One that I can understand why girls would melt for it. "Big guy might wanna work on his hospitality."

"That's what I'm here for," I reply and prepare to turn around when his voice stops me.

"Melody."

The softness of his tone weakens my knees.

Nope. Get it together Melody. You have a job to do!

"Can I call you, Mel?" The request seems harmless.

No such thing in this lifestyle.

"Sure." This time I turn all the way around to hide the reddening in my face.

"I'm Drew."

"McCoy, I know," I assure him as I start to place the food I won't be cooking at this moment in the fridge.

"You say that like there's a stigma to my last name."

The accusation causes me to shake my head.

"So you're saying there's nothing wrong with me being a McCoy?"

"Other than being in the top five people The Devil hates? No."

His chuckle causes me to glance over my shoulder again. At the sight of my face he shrugs. "Guess I'll consider myself lucky."

"That's luck?"

"Rather be in top five of his enemies than the top five of his so called friends."

Puzzled by the thought, I lean against the counter. "Why?"

"At least as an enemy you won't be blindsided by the bullet coming at you." He pauses and stares me deep in the eyes.

Do you see those brown eyes? Holy hell they're mesmerizing.

"And with a man like that, there's always a bullet coming for you, so called friend or foe. When you're the latter you at least know to be prepared."

I wish he was wrong. I wish I could say that that wasn't true. That I don't have to worry about my life being 'on his side', but it would be a lie. An easy lie to spot. An even harder one to live.

Doing my best to keep the conversation away from my employer I ask, "Hungry?"

He counters, "Where are we, Mel?"

"In a cottage."

"Where?"

"I can't disclose that information."

Drew scratches the side of his neck. "Can I speak to my brother again?"

"You will be given one chance to speak to Madden and Destin together. Then one final call will be had with The Devil and Daniel the day of the job."

He slides the cigarette behind his ear before shoving his hands in his pockets. "Why would he let me talk to my other brothers? Kindness isn't his style."

"Insurance."

"Excuse me?"

"He will show them proof of life, so they will continue to keep their mouths shut. The Devil exploits the emotion known as hope. He gives someone a glimmer of hope and uses it to manipulate them into complying with his wishes."

Before you ask how you beat something like that...I'll tell you. It's simple really. Give. Up. Hope. Like I did years ago.

"You're not allergic to eggs, but do you like them?"

My subject change has his head tilting. "What?"

"Eggs. They come from chickens. Do you like eggs? I was going to make them and some pancakes. Maybe some sausage for breakfast?"

Drew nods slowly. "I like eggs..."

Pleased the change worked, I turn back around, almost done putting the groceries away. "Good."

"How'd you know I'm not allergic?"

I shut my eyes, thankful my back is to him. "It was...it was in the file I read."

"There's a file on me?"

"There's files on most of The Devil's employees and clients."

"Why?"

"Leverage," is my breathless response. Still not wanting to have to confess the evil ways of a man, I loathe but have to obey, into deep brown eyes that could turn a girl into putty, I shut the fridge door and stare at the stainless steel instead. "He takes know thy enemy very seriously."

"So there's one on you?"

The loaded question doesn't get answered.

There's a file alright. It's filled with more than the fact I have a mild shellfish allergy. It's got the kind of information that if I were ever turned over to the authorities there would be very little hesitation with giving me a lethal injection.

Drew

While chewing I keep my eyes alert to everything possible.

Just because I'm trapped like a lab rat doesn't mean I can't be aware of my surroundings. While I was outside having a smoke I did a small scan of the yard, but I'll admit, it was hard to stare at anything other than the gorgeous girl making me breakfast. Melody. Even her name sounds fucking sweet. Imagine how beautiful she'll sound falling apart for me. How her orgasmic cries will be my new lullaby.

Spotting another one, I lean back in my chair and ask, "What's with all the cameras? They're fucking everywhere."

"You learn to get used to them," Melody hums before sucking syrup off her pinky.

Just because my dick is way bigger than that doesn't mean her mouth wouldn't make similar motions. It just means her perfect lips would be parted wider and the pleased hum would be louder. Oh, don't give me lectures about how wrong it is to be concerned with getting my dick touched while I'm being held captive. Trust me. I know. But a woman this beautiful plays tricks with the mind.

I adjust my growing hard on. "Oh yeah?"

"Yeah." Suddenly she scoots her chair closer to me, hunches forward, and insists by eyebrow movements that I repeat her action. As soon as I do, she whispers, "It's all about angles. The cameras are more for show than for tell. No audio. More like a reminder put in place that you are being watched rather than to actually watch you. For most people that thought alone is enough."

Not being able to help myself, I smile. "Not for you?"

"It stopped being enough years ago," she answers.

Concerned I ask, "How long have you lived here?"

"Under The Devil's thumb or the cottage?"

"Both."

"About four years."

"That's a long time not to know freedom," I reply softly grabbing one of the sausage links.

"You would know."

The comment causes me to nod.

We weren't even legal when we started assisting Madden with The Devil's work. Being so young we were easy to manipulate and buy every bullshit illusion he promised us. He delivered the miles of women, the mountains of money, and the endless jobs that pushed the envelope, but eventually all good things have to come end and blood started being spilled. Sadly, I don't think it's done being spilled.

Slyly I compliment, "Those pancakes were amazing by the way."

Melody reaches for her orange juice. "Thanks."

"Growing up, big breakfasts like this were a rare thing. We were kinda poor, but mom could make pancakes stretch on a budget. She used to put a dash of cinnamon and a pinch of sugar." Recalling the mornings of stuffing as many of those thin objects I could in my mouth causes me to smile wider. "We didn't always have syrup, so when we didn't, she would just add more sugar."

There's a brush of her leg against mine, dragging my eyes to hers. "I add a drizzle of chocolate syrup. Helps kill the need to wanna add more syrup than necessary."

"Smart woman."

"Not really," she sighs. "It's just science."

Baffled by the left field comment I grab my milk glass. "Oh yeah? What makes you say that?"

"Because it's science," she repeats. "It's just the simple action of balancing the body's sugar levels.

"How would you know? You're not a chemist. A hell of a chef, but not a chemist."

Melody toys with the end of her braid but doesn't argue.

No...no fucking way.

"You're a fucking chemist?"

"Not exactly..."

"What do you mean not exactly?"

"I mean my lab isn't in a building where people need a badge to enter and exit. I don't get to wear a white lab coat and have people see my accomplishments plastered on my wall. I mix compounds that yield necessary and desired results for a man who proves the line between genius and sociopath is indeed a thin one."

For a moment I don't respond. I simply stare at the saddened expression on her face, the way her cheeks that were heated by our casual touch seconds before are now pale, proving to me, this is no more her home than it is mine. Her jail sentence here is just longer than mine.

We'll see about that.

"Your ass wouldn't look good covered in a coat."

Immediately taken off guard by my words her face flushes again.

"However, I would be okay with fucking you on one of those counters." The color deepens and I add, "As long as there are no lab rats around. Those would kinda kill the mood."

Melody starts giggling covering her mouth to keep the incredible sound from being exposed. Casually I brush my leg against hers.

A little flirting never hurt. I'm not dumb enough to think fucking her would allow me to escape any faster...Doesn't mean I can't enjoy my cell mate.

"You have a beautiful laugh."

She turns to look at me. "I don't get many chances for other people to hear it to know if that's true or not." As if some realization has hit her, she stands, keeping her face down. Melody grabs her dishes. "Are you done?"

"Yeah," I answer unsure how I screwed that up. "I can help with-"

"No." Her voice coldly states. "It would be best if you started on your task." My mouth twitches to object when she informs, "I will clear the table and give you a clean work space. Feel free to take a moment and get washed up. You will be able to start momentarily."

And just like that, the brief warmness that was appearing has faded away behind dark clouds again.

This is going to be the longest two weeks of my life. I just pray at the end of it all, I can free more than just myself.

Melody

It's weird the way he keeps staring at me, right? Look at him! Look at the way the end of that pencil is tucked between his teeth while his eyes glance at me! That's weird. I know I haven't been around men who would find me sexually appealing in years, but that doesn't mean that that's what that look has to be.

I check the clock on my phone once more knowing there's about another hour before I have to start The Devil's latest request.

Drew's voice invades my thoughts. "So how did The Devil know I could sculpt?"

"It's in your file."

"Just a note like 'Oh hey he can sculpt if necessary'? Or something like a list of the classes I took in high school?"

The question rubs me the wrong way, so I don't reply.

Ya know, I'm not the secretary. It's not my job to keep the records. That's someone else's doing. How the hell am I supposed to know? To be fair I've wondered the same thing. I'm dying to know what little tid bits about myself are just waiting to be used against me again.

Suddenly Drew stands, pencil and paper still in his hand, as he heads towards me. "Does it have the story about Clarissa Walkins?"

Confused, but curious, I look up from book I was trying to read. "Who?"

With a soft smirk he flops down on the off white couch beside me. He crosses his leg to continue to use it as a table, his knee grazing mine once more. The sensation, which shouldn't send so much as a second thought to my brain breaks my skin out in goosebumps again.

It's been a really long time since I've had contact like that. Well, real contact. I've had the touch of the dead, the close to it, and the unconscious more times than I can count, but the last time someone with a pulse, someone with their eyes open, touched me is lost with so many other memories. Omar is protective and father like, but he doesn't touch me in any way. No hugs. Nothing. Do you know what lack of touch can do to the human mind? Trust me. You don't wanna find out.

"She was this girl in my Math class," he starts to explain, pencil still moving across the sheet of paper.

Instead of watching the drawing, I watch Drew. There's something so striking about him, it's hard not to.

Shh. It could be that I haven't been around a male like this in quite some time or it could be the way all the features on his face are dark, while his skin is an enticing shade lighter creating a contrast. Part of me thinks it's the light brown eyes that seem to be twinkling even now. Even in this hell hole. How is that possible?

"Clarissa had a thing for jocks. Believe it or not, I wasn't a huge fan." His light chuckle lets the one that leaves me feel safe. "However, she did have a thing for custom jewelry. One of a kind shit. So in sculpting class, I carved her out this little tear drop shape, found a shiny rock and put it inside. Created her this amazing piece, had one of my brothers cop me a chain for it and gave it to her."

"She like it?"

There's a smug smirk on his face. "She fucking loved it."

Wouldn't you?

"Her boyfriend however...not so much."

A gasp comes out of my mouth that forces his face upward.

"Did I forget to mention that at the beginning of the story?"

"A little," I whisper.

He shrugs in the way that I'm seeing is signature for him. One shoulder and a head tilt. "Wasn't a big deal to me."

"Because you like a challenge?"

"You know, easy girls are just that. Easy. Challenges, are never about the person involved, but the struggle of power." His eyes latch onto mine refusing to let them go. "I prefer mutual attraction." My legs unconsciously move closer together. Drew's leg jumps on the idea of gravitating towards them. "Call me old fashion."

Trying to hide my blush, I simply fiddle with my braid. The river of heat scorching its way through my veins causes me to rub my chest a little in hopes of clearing the passage way for air to cool down my body.

It's just his fucking leg! I'm crazy...

"What um...what happened between you and the girl?"

"She left him for me." He smiles widely. "Did you really see that story ending differently?"

I chuckle and shake my head. "You're arrogant."

His tongue moistens his lips. "I'm accurate."

Only a little bit of me wonders what he tastes like. Not enough for you to bring it up.

"If it makes up for it, he started to trash her around school, so I sculpted a tiny dick statue and engraved underneath it 'Christopher Dallas' Dick. Object is a replica of actual size.'" My eyes widen. "I then had Clarissa leave it in the girls locker room where it remained until he graduated." In disbelief I start giggling and shaking my head. "We didn't actually date that long. Turns out she had her own agenda too. She wanted to know what made the McCoys so legendary. It didn't take long before I lost interest. There's something about dating chicks that want you just for your name."

"Um...don't all the girls you hook up with want you because of that?"

"Yeah. That's why we hook up." He points his pencil at me matter of factly. "Not date."

"You don't date?"

Drew shakes his head. "Not in years."

The direction of the conversation is one I want to push, but know I shouldn't.

It's none of my business. None of this is. Yeah, I'm curious too, but there's a saying about that. Remember what happened to the cat?

"I haven't sculpted in almost just as long."

"You've got just a little time to practice."

"Yeah..." He adjusts the paper tablet, which knocks his leg against me, and ignites the goosebumps all over again. "What about you? Can you sculpt?"

Sheepishly I shake my head. "I can't even draw stick figures."

He chuckles. "Everyone can draw stick figure people."

"No. Not everyone."

"Everyone."

"I swear. They either look like anorexic snowflakes or mini Michelin men."

Drew holds the pencil out for me. I give him a sarcastic look before shaking my head. "Oh come on. You can't say shit like that and not expect me to ask you to deliver."

Don't agree with him!

Giggling I shake my head again. "No."

"Yes."

"No."

"Yes."

"No, which means no."

"No is just a substitute for those waiting for a reason to say yes."

The description causes my jaw to drop. "What am I waiting for?"

Drew leans over so his lips are feathering my ear. "Me." Without pausing for my permission my body melts against him. "Do it for me Mel."

Instinctively I prepare to deny one last time.

Softly he adds, "Please."

His words roll around in my brain doing their best to separate the actual meaning from the innuendo I wish he was referring to. On a soft sigh, I snatch the pencil. "Fine. But you asked for this monstrosity."

He nods as I lean over, so my body is pressed tightly against his. Unsure if the closeness is necessary or not, I take it for what it is. Happening. I do my best to focus on the request, my hand shaking while the creation falls in the empty corner on the page. When I'm finally finished there's a sense of pride sitting on my shoulders.

Not too bad, huh?

"That's....that's..." Drew seems to struggle to find the words. "That's awful."

I hate him.

"Well," I snap and shove the pencil back at him. "I tried to warn you."

"Is that supposed to be a snowman on a diet?"

"Shut up."

"Did he confuse cocaine for snow?" The teasing continues until I start to smile. "Should we all be on this diet?"

"Very funny." Rolling my eyes, I make the motion to move away when Drew's body tenses as if indicating it wants me to stay right where I am. Nervously I swallow. "I tried to tell you."

His arm extends around the back of the couch.

It makes me wonder if he could wrap his arm around me right now would he. What do you mean of course he would?

"Can you draw a heart?"

"So you can tell me that it looks like a pumpkin exploded or something. No."

"I won't say that."

A sarcastic scowl comes from me.

"Swear." He surrenders his left hand. "I won't say that. Draw me a heart."

"Why?"

"Just trust me?"

I shake my head.

I learned my lesson trusting a gorgeous smile and a smooth talker a very long time ago.

"I wanna show you something. Draw the heart."

A deep sigh escapes me. I snatch the pencil back from him. I concentrate with everything in me on drawing the simple curves and trying to connect them at a point. Once I'm fairly certain I've done an alright job, I offer him back the pencil. I expect him to take it with his right, but he uses his left. He proceeds to shade my heart, turning it from a simple doodle into something remarkable. Suddenly it has veins and valves like an actual beating organ. Next thing I know there are pulse lines coming out of it to make the letter M.

"This is a tattoo all of Triple D has," he announces as he finishes. "Destin designed it. He designed most of the tattoos we have, but this one was to represent our mom. She was the heartbeat of the McCoys. She uh...she never hesitated to do what it took to keep us safe."

I look over with just enough time to see a sadness I can relate to. Wanting to go where I know I don't need to, I once again redirect our attention, fighting the instinct to attach myself to the first new object in my fishbowl of a life. "You drew that with your left hand."

A little smirk returns to his hardened face. "Yeah. Daniel's fucking left handed, so it became a skill I had to learn. That's the thing when you're always switching places. Smarter people pay attention to little details like that."

"So you can sculpt...and Destin can draw?"

"He can. He rarely does it anymore," he mumbles more to himself than me, the pencil still darkening the lines. "Merrick could paint."

My body nestles a little closer. His fingers drop to my shoulder where he lightly strokes. "So, you're all slightly artistic?"

"No." The answer causes him to laugh to himself. He lifts his head up still smiling. "Madden and Daniel's art skills are about as great as yours." I playfully elbow him, which causes him to laugh more. "Daniel has an insane ability to spot a vehicle and give you it's face value worth from what you would just assume was a glance. Let him get a really good look at it and most of the time he can nail it within the five dollar range."

"Impressive."

"Handy when people think they can fuck you over," he explains. "Madden on the other hand, has an unreal way of identifying the make, model, and year of a vehicle from sound. I know how fucking bizarre that sounds, but it's true. He says all cars have a different tune, a different frequency. It's like some next level super human shit."

"You McCoys are all super humans," I mumble.

Oh shit. I shouldn't have said that.

"What's that supposed to mean?"

I shake my head and drop my face forward.

"Mel," his voice gingerly calls to me. "Mel, look at me."

Immediately my body complies.

Damn it. See one of the downfalls of not having human contact? The first time I get it, my body wants to submit to anything requested from it.

"Tell me."

In a hushed tone I reply, "Because look at how you live. Look how long you've lived that way and never been caught by the cops."

"I'd rather be caught by the cops than The Devil any day."

"Me too," my mouth whispers, a tear crawling it's way down my throat, attempting to close it off. Feeling the air in the room being sucked out, I stand up. Space will be a good thing. Moving will be even better. I head for the kitchen. "Sandwiches okay for lunch?"

Drew clears his throat. "Works for me."

Silence fills the cottage and I'm thankful.

This is probably for the best. The more I talk to him, the more likeliness guilt over all of this will settle in and make it even harder for me to sleep at night. As it is, I already have to take a sleeping aid most nights. The last thing I really need is another excuse to up the dosage. After the last hostage I had to care for, it took ten days before I could fall asleep without thoughts of suicide. She was a sweet girl. She was also The Police Commissioner's daughter caught up in a world she never asked to be in. She reminded me of myself. Yeah...I've gotta detach myself from him. This is gonna end so much worse than that did. She got to walk away from it all at the end.

"Mel," his voice is now directly over my shoulder. The heat of his body close to mine has my eyes shutting. Drew's hands land on the counter on each side of me, trapping my body beside his. "Who's watching those cameras?"

In an unsteady voice, I confess, "No one."

"No one?"

"I told you," I whimper as his scent invades my senses, his lips now close to my ear again. "They're...um...they're more for show than tell. The Devil records it, but unless given a reason he doesn't watch them."

The pressure from his body increases as his lips seem to nudge my ear once more. "Is it bad I wanna be the reason he does?"

His attempt at flirtation stops my actions completely. Concern has me spin around in his arms, his face now distractingly close.

Wow. That's....right. Focus.

"Is getting me into bed about giving The Devil a fuck you from captivity or actually being attracted to me?"

Drew's face twitches and for a moment, I'm not sure he even considered one of those a possibility before I mentioned it.

The problem is I'm not certain which one.

He takes a step back to answer, but is cut off.

"Melody," Omar's voice sternly says from the entry way. "Are you ready?"

I meet Omar's eyes and inform him, "You're early."

"Is that a problem?" he almost growls. "Am I interrupting something?"

"Yeah," Drew responds. With the cocky smirk he typically has he answers, "Lunch."

"Make your own fucking lunch," Omar bites.

"*I* will finish making him lunch, but I still have to grab some shit from Eden-"

"What's Eden?" Drew intrudes.

"My garden." Before he can make a smart comment I say to Omar, "Twenty minutes tops."

"Fine." He sheds his jacket and heads for the couch. "I'll wait here."

Drew mutters, "Joy..."

With a roll of the eyes, I turn back around to return to making him a sandwich. Quietly, but professionally I instruct, "Please have a seat at the table McCoy and I'll bring you your meal shortly."

He doesn't object or even add a comment. He simply does as requested.

Thank God. I don't need Omar to have any more reason to question me than he already is. The problem is, now I see what Omar saw the second Drew walked into my world. I can't say that I blame him for reacting the way he did. He doesn't want me to die any more than I want me to, but if I don't get my shit together, what we want and what will happen will not be the same thing.

Melody

Omar clears his throat at me indicating he wants me to look at him. I continue to keep my attention out the window.

There's nothing good about looking at him right now. I'm not in any mood. I just...I wanna be left alone.

"Melody."

"Don't," I mutter and smile at the sight of a little girl brushing her doll's hair in the backseat of her mother's van, which is beside us at the stop light. "Just...don't."

He mumbles something to himself, but I ignore it. The little girl with blonde pig tails looks up at me and waves. Her innocence is beautiful and refreshing. I wiggle my finger back at her. She giggles before she returns to her doll leaving me with a new reason for tears to clog my throat.

I'll never get to have kids. I'll never get to be a mini-van mom. There will never be a child that relies on me to keep their innocence. I know that's probably for the best, but it doesn't make it hurt any less. I'll never get to nag at her about letting me brush her hair or fight a fussy baby boy who won't sit still enough for me to feed him. Every time I get a glimpse of a future I can never have, my anxiety levels shift and ending my own life lands on the table once more.

"Are you doing your job?"

My eyes shut as I rest my forehead against the window. "Yes."

"Does he know?"

I shake my head.

Please don't ask me. It's bad enough I have to do it without talking about it.

"Good," Omar hums.

"Good?" I gripe back.

"I'd rather you keep your life than him."

In a soft plea I sigh, "What makes my life any more valuable than his?"

"Because I care about you."

"And he has an entire family that cares about him," I argue.

"That doesn't fucking matter to me." Omar states. "The McCoys are nothing more than another pair of hands The Devil uses when he doesn't wanna dirty his own. They mean nothing. They are nothing. They're disposable."

My head slowly turns to face him. "You know that's what The Devil said about Jimmy?" When Omar nods, I shake my head. "Was it true then?"

"Yes." His coldness doesn't surprise me, but saddens me. "And it's true now. Men like them are like tissues. Use them and get rid of them. People like you and me, we're necessary. We're needed."

"Until we're not," I conclude, the conversation I had with Drew this morning now haunting as the car pulls to a stop outside of a warehouse by the docks.

Before getting out of the vehicle, I grab the case I've been sent to deliver. Walking along side Omar, I straighten my posture, hold my head up, and hide any insecurities that were lingering.

When The Devil smells fear, he smells weakness, and when he smells that, your remaining life span immediately is cut in half.

Omar delivers a sharp bang on the garage door. "Open."

The door rises just enough for us to duck under. Inside we take just a few steps before The Devil appears from around the corner with a pleasant expression on his face.

You should be afraid. Trust me.

He extends his hands in a welcoming motion. "Ah....Eve."

The nickname, which is meant to be a compliment as much as it is a curse causes me to nod at him. "Afternoon."

"Did you bring me a present?" I nod, which causes the demonic smirk to stretch harshly across his face. "Excellent."

Omar and I cross to him. Immediately I offer him the case and sigh, "Is that all you need?"

He stares at me for a moment before looking up at Omar who is expressionless. Unsure of how he senses it, I know he's latched onto the tension. "Why don't you come watch the results of your beloved work first hand?" My mouth twitches in objection, but I know better than to actually do that. Like the demon incarnate he is, he wiggles his eyebrows, "Come along. You'll love it."

I won't. There's no way I ever will. I'm not the monster he is...I swear. I know that's hard to believe with what I do for a living, but just...try to believe me.

The two of us follow him around the corner down a hallway into a wide cleared out space. Inside it is a man, bloodied, bruised, and barely recognizable. He's hanging from a hook that's dropped down from the ceiling. Seeing this causes my stomach to boil and flesh to crawl, just as it always does when he feels the need to remind me not only what he's capable of, but what he does daily.

Fear is almost as powerful as hope. Both can shake a person to their core.

Strolling away from us, The Devil heads towards him, the case dangling from his fingertips. "Do you know what's in here?"

The injured man shakes his head.

One of The Devil's men who had been assisting the roughing up of the man acts as a table for his employer. He extends his arms out to hold the case while The Devil opens it. "I had Eve bring me something special."

Tempted to look away, to look anywhere else, I dig my fingernails into my arm and look straight on.

I have to give him what he expects or risk being next.

"This," he begins by holding up the small vial of clear liquid. "Well this little beauty is very dangerous. See, it's going to paralyze your body from moving while enhancing your sensitivity to pain. Basically a prick which might not even register to you is going to feel like someone is stabbing you with a katana."

The man begs, "Please..."

"I wasn't finished," The Devil snaps. "After your pain sensors have been heightened to the max your organs will begin to shut down within the next couple of hours. One...by...one...until you're dead on this hook like the worm you are." Aggressively he grabs the man's face. "And you're a fucking worm. A useless maggot Cash." The Devil spits in his face. "Now tell me who the fuck is selling out my men left and right!"

Cash begins to blubber like a man at the end of his rope. A man with his life flashing before his eyes. A man who knows no matter what he does or does not say, it's not going to matter. He's going to die.

"You're one of the only pieces of shit left they haven't come for. I find that fucking convenient. A little suspicious."

"The McCoys..."

"Haven't stepped foot in or out of that building since this shit started to happen," he announces. "We've reviewed the footage. All the angles, inside and out. No one has seen them anywhere near the building. They aren't narking me out, but someone is." The Devil grabs the needle and begins to fill it. "You know what I call this little mixture Eve made me?" With a sadistic smirk he looks over his shoulder. "Do you remember?"

I dig my nails into my flesh tighter. The rest of my body remains still.

"Hail Mary," he hums proudly tossing the empty vial back into the case. "Because that's the only fucking chance you have at escaping." The Devil doesn't wait for Cash to say anything else before jamming the shot in the man's neck and injecting all the poison.

There's a sharp cry from the man before The Devil tosses the needle the same way he did the vial. Sharply he turns and begins to walk away while the muscle that wasn't holding the case returns to torturing the man.

Closer to me, The Devil adjusts his cuffs. Looking at his assistant, who I had no idea arrived on the other side of Omar, he questions, "Is this blood on my cuff?"

Vicki, his assistant for so many things, leans forward. "Yes."

He drops his head backwards. "I hate trying to get blood stains out of my clothes." The moment he lifts his face back up, he cocks a smile. "I think I want a giraffe..." He pauses briefly before nodding. "I'm gonna get one. Eve, is there anything you need for Eden."

Barely audible I answer, "No."

He smiles widely as he takes the cigar from Vicki, his attention now wrapped around her instead of me. "You think it'll be expensive?"

Her reply is lost upon me while I stare forward as my only purpose in his life settles in the veins of a potentially innocent man.

How do I live with myself? Honestly? I wonder the same thing most days. And if I'm being completely truthful, I'm not sure how much longer I can.

Drew

You know what I hate about clay? No matter how much I try to get this shit off my body it finds a crevice to hide in. No joke. I showered last night, scrubbed myself so hard you would think I might've used a brillo pad, only to find it dried in random places on my skin. Fucking hate clay...

Slightly groggy, I stretch through the aches in my body.

That's new too. Part of me wonders if it's because of the mattress. I feel like that princess who couldn't sleep with a pea under mattress. Did I really just call myself a princess? Wow. If you see my testicles that I lost while I was sleeping could you kick 'em back over please?

I head for the bathroom with a slight limp in the leg that was grazed.

It hadn't been hurting, but it is this morning. Strange. That's probably normal. I was grazed by a bullet.

Turning on the light in the small luxury bathroom, I immediately turn my attention to the slight discoloration of my skin near the injury. Confused on what the hell that's about I lift my leg onto the marble counter and stare.

Unsure of how long I've been poking at the area, I'm startled by a voice. "Gym stretches?"

I look over at Melody who's in a pair of white scrubs with her hair freshly braided. She's holding a glass of water and two pills out for me.

Casually I drop my leg back to the ground. "Aren't you supposed to stay fit in prison?" Instead of giving her a chance to take that the wrong way, I quickly add, "At least that's how it is in the movies. Every prison movie...ever..."

She giggles and shrugs. "I wouldn't know."

"You don't watch movies?"

Melody's cheer instantly dissolves into somberness.

Fuck. I gotta figure out how to stop doing that. Yesterday I was trying to kiss her...yeah hold all judgments on falling for the girl who is holding you hostage against her own will please...and managed to get my own foot in my mouth. That never happens outside this place yet with her it keeps happening. What the hell is wrong with me?

"No. Not in years," she softly answers. Clearing her throat she offers the contents of her hands again. "Take these. They'll help with the pain."

I grab the glass and down the two pills. "Is the discoloring in my leg-"

"Normal? Yes. It's just healing. Oddly, but considering how you were stitched up, there's nothing to worry about. I'll check for infection again tomorrow."

Nodding I lean my ass against the counter. "So you're a doctor now too?"

She reaches for the glass. "I'm a lot of things, Drew."

Quickly I move the glass out of the way. "Beautiful should be at the top of the list."

There's a brief blush on her cheeks. With a simple shake of her head, she bats it away. "Glass, please?"

I scoot over and hold it higher. "Are you in a hurry?"

She huffs and looks up at the object just out of her reach. "A bit."

"To run off again?" I question. "You didn't even return before I crashed."

"I wasn't aware you were keeping tabs on me," she snips and folds her arms across her chest. "That's actually *my job* while you're here."

I smirk. "Doesn't mean, I can't do the same."

"Give me the glass, Drew."

Nonchalantly I shake my head. She moves further in the bathroom to reach for it again.

Oh I know exactly what I'm doing. Don't call me a child.

"There aren't cameras in here," I state slowly. "How come?"

"Because there's audio."

Baffled how that makes sense I toss my hand in the air waiting for her to explain.

"False privacy tactic. You think you're safe. You might slip up and make a mistake. Say something you wouldn't have when cameras were watching. No. He doesn't listen to it any more than he watches the tapes. Like I said, unless he's given a reason, it's more for show than anything else." She moves towards me again. "Now, glass."

When I pretend to lower the glass, she takes the bait. Swiftly I wrap an arm around her waist and guide her against the wall that's opposite of the entry way. As soon as her back hits it, I drop my lips on top of hers. Like I expected she fights back, a hand banging at my chest while her lips don't try to deceive. They fall apart, inviting more of me in. I use the hand that's slipped around her back to pull her into me as I lean backwards to feel for the counter space for the glass. The second it's out of my possession, I use my other hand to support myself against the wall. With it stretched out, and my other hand tugging her into me as she tries to put on a facade of escape, I get lost into the rife waves of ecstasy.

I've kissed enough chicks to the point where after the initial moment, there's nothing left to be surprised by. Nothing left to thrill someone that's seen it all. Well...almost seen it all, it seems. I could kiss this chick forever. That's something I damn sure haven't had before.

She whimpers and pushes at my shoulder, which pulls my lips from hers. Melody stares at me, her azure eyes glazed over with a look I've seen a million times, but never been more thankful to as I am now. Slowly her head moves back and forth. I use the hand that was lingering on her hip to stroke her cheek. Her eyes lazily close. I take the invitation to return our tongues together, this time even more feverishly. Desperate to consume as much of her as I can in this one moment, this one moment I may never get again, I offer up my kisses like an oblation to this goddess who is just as imprisoned as I am.

To my surprise Melody grips the waist band of my boxers until my body is flush with hers. My dick nudges towards the heat radiating from her.

Can you blame him? He just better not come. If I bust a nut from the idea of this shit alone there's no reattaching my balls.

For only a moment longer, we remain lost in a whirlwind of tongues, touches, and the temptation to moan our delight and desire for more.

When she pulls back this time, she touches her swollen lips, regret as prevalent as excitement. Pushing past me, she grabs the glass and doesn't say another word. She shuts the door once she's on the other side, leaving my body in a state of distress that almost matches what's going on in my mind.

I pull back the shower curtain and start the water. In one easy motion, I'm naked and under the water, dick in my eager hand that's more than ready to help me find some relief. Letting my head hit the space under the shower, the warm water rolls across my shoulders acting as a pathetic replacement for the warmth I'm seeking. It doesn't stop my hand or my mind from pretending it's something else. Suddenly the image of Mel naked, hands wrapping around my waist floods my mind, causing me to leak out the groans I couldn't before. The thought of her soft hand wrapped around my cock, jerking me back and forth, feels like I've stumbled upon the keys to the castle. The path to the ultimate fucking orgasm. In my mind she strokes faster, hand occasionally giving my nuts a tug. Each time her palm rubs against my ampallang piercing I let out another moan. At the moment they're so close together that it feels like I'm no longer breathing, I come hard, the fluid falling down the drain. Struggling to capture my breath, I keep my eyes closed, the fact that I shouldn't be thinking about sex at a time like this is irrelevant.

Look, there's no escaping before the heist is to be completed. That's a fact. When the chance comes, I won't miss it. And if I can, I'm gonna free her too. Free her and bring her home to my bed where I will show her a life she hasn't been able to see in years. Keep showing her how good life should be. Keep sharing my life with her. My word.

Once I'm dry and in pair of fresh sweat pants, I stroll out of my room to where Melody is putting breakfast on the round kitchen table.

Without looking at me she announces. "Omelets."

"Are there veggies in them?"

Puzzled, she looks at me. "No...do you...do you not like vegetables?"

Flopping down in the wooden chair, I answer, "Not for breakfast."

"Why not?"

"Do I look like Popeye to you?"

The joke works. Melody lets out a priceless laugh and another wall from her resistance fort comes down.

Hey, the sooner she realizes I'm not here to hurt her, but help her, the better.

"You grow all your own vegetables, don't you?" She nods as she hands me a napkin. "Is that what makes your garden special enough to be called Eden?"

Slowly she shakes her head in denial before having a seat. "It's so much more than that."

"Oh yeah?" I pick up my fork. "Will you show me?"

Melody's face tries not to smile. "Maybe."

"Maybe is better than no."

"Which is what people say while waiting for a reason to say yes," she quotes.

Oh yeah. A girl who can throw my words back at me? How could I not wanna keep her?

After a chuckle I start in on my breakfast. Each bite, somehow, taste better than the last.

I've never fucking had eggs this good before. It shouldn't even be humanly possible to make them taste like this. No, you can't have a bite.

"What else is in the garden? Just flowers and shit?"

She leans back in her chair, eyes falling on me. "That too. Herbs. Plants that can be broken down to make different pharmaceutical needs. Ointments. Poisons. Antidotes."

If she can do all that shit, why hasn't she poisoned The Devil yet? I mean, yeah it's probably not that easy. Chances are if she tried and failed, he'd kill her on the spot. Knowing how his fucking mind works, he'd probably spot the idea a mile away. Well, I bet the thought has at least crossed her mind.

"How do you even get started learning that shit?"

Melody offers me a wide smile this time. "Plants are easier to get along with than people."

I chuckle. "That's how my big brother feels about cars."

She giggles.

Fuck I love that sound.

"Given that you think being Queen of the Amazon is easier than Queen of the Social Pyramid, what else spurred you to wanna...be Poison Ivy?"

When she laughs again, this time her head falls back and the smallest snort comes out of her. "A Batman reference, really?"

"So you do know movies?"

"Old ones," she sheepishly confesses.

"Well when I get you the fuck out of this place, updating you on those will definitely be on the list of things to do."

Melody doesn't acknowledge the declaration. "My father died of an overdose. I wondered why. Wondered how. I had an early interest in chemical compound break downs like that. I graduated high school early, started college at 17, was almost done with my master's degree when I ended up...here."

"Wait. Wait. Wait. How the fuck is that possible? College is like four years!"

"I started taking college credits as freshman. Went to summer school. Did courses online. Wasn't that hard."

"Wasn't that hard?" I snap. "Are you joking?"

"Studying came natural to me. I didn't have a lot of friends-"

"Boyfriends?"

Her mouth opens to say something, but she hesitates.

Why do I feel like she was going to deny any body would wanna date her? If she said that we all know it would be a lie. Look at her. No. Seriously, look at her. She's could easily be a porn star with the way her body is stacked and a makeup ad model with her perfect complexion. Come on.

"I didn't have that problem." Before I can ask any more questions, she picks her fork back up and asks, "What about you? Did you always know it was cars and motorcycles for you?"

I hum and reach for my juice. "That's one way of putting it. We were never really given a choice to consider other options. Madden needed more hands in the shop. He wanted a family business. We had always had an attraction for cars 'cause of our dad and bikes 'cause of our uncle, so it seemed to fit. College was never on the agenda."

Melody questions, "Do you wish it was?"

My eyes cut over to her, hands still wrapped around the glass.

"Do you wish it would've been an option? I mean...if it had been, you wouldn't be here."

In a whisper I confess, "I don't know that I *don't* wanna be here."

Immediately her face starts to burn bright once more.

"Yeah, being held hostage, not exactly the ideal way of meeting the girl of your dreams, but I think what matters is *actually* meeting her."

Oh yeah. That...that totally sounded like a line. Shut up! Let me fix it.

With a slow head shake she pushes her barely eaten meal away from her. "Drew, I'm not who you think I am."

"Let me ask you something." I mimic her last action. "If The Devil granted you your freedom, no consequences, no repercussions for walking away from him, would you go?"

She turns her head towards me to nod.

"Exactly." Under the table I let my hand slowly slide across her thigh to her hand that's lingering in her lap. "You're just as much a prisoner as I am. Your chains may not be the same, your sentence may be a little longer, but you don't belong here anymore than I do."

Instead of pushing me away like I expect, she folds her fingers with mine, an ease washing over her. Seeing the softness blanket her causes a tranquility to invade my own body unexpectedly.

What the fuck is that? Side effect of the pain killers?

In a whisper she confides, "You're the first person to touch me like this in years."

"Good," I reply.

She scoffs. "Good?"

"Yeah." My hand squeezes hers tighter. "I honestly hate the idea of *anyone* touching you that isn't me."

Her bottom lip slips between her teeth.

"About that kiss..."

"You regret it?"

"Fuck no." The quick response causes her to jump slightly. "I just wanted to say, I wasn't finished when you walked away."

Melody giggles and shakes her head. "I had to."

"And I have to finish what I started. I'm not a man who likes to leave projects unfinished."

"Is that what I am?" A cold expression crosses her face. "A project? Something to toy with to help pass the time by?"

"Finding each and every way I can make you whimper from pleasure is a project I don't take lightly." Her mouth leaks out a small moan. "I'm not looking to just pass the time by with you, Mel. I'm looking to make the time with you mean something." When her mouth shuts I add, "And I think you know that. And I think that's why you run. Because getting attached to something frightens you-"

"Because everything around me dies," she blurts.

Comforting...

"I'm not gonna die," I assure her. "Not here. Not on this bullshit mission for The Devil. I guarantee that."

Melody looks away obviously not convinced.

Don't join her. Trust me here. I mean, I can see how you'd be a little skeptical, but I'm telling you. Have a little more faith.

Abruptly she drops my hand and stands. She reaches for the dishes. "If you're finished with your breakfast, you need to get started for the day."

I nod. "I am but-"

"Hand me your plate please." Once I oblige, she turns with both dishes in her hand. "I'll be out of your way shortly. Dishes and then I'll be in Eden if you need anything."

Unsure of why she's trying to push me away again, I stare straight ahead out the window that's showing the gorgeous sight of the backyard area. "How will I contact you if I do?"

"There are intercoms all around the house. Find one."

Keeping my back to her I continue to admire the way the green grass seems to stretch for miles, a dark forest area appearing to be much closer than it actually is.

Well if that isn't a fucking metaphor I don't know what is. I just hope whatever darkness Mel is hiding from me will eventually let my light touch it.

Melody

Oh yeah. I'm fucked. Royally fucked. I thought that kiss was a mistake. I thought that would be the ultimate 'I'm making a terrible choice' mistake, but I was wrong. Oh so wrong! All that kiss has done is spur me to keep making mistakes. To keep putting myself in a position I can't make it out of. But you know what? I'm tired of not being alive. I used to think as long as there was air in my lungs I was living. That as long as I woke up and went to sleep, that's all that mattered. Another day was won as best as it could be. I used to think all the tragic shit that happened in between was just one more tally on the long list of shit I needed forgiveness for at the gates of Heaven and as long as I made it to the end of the road, I was okay. My life had been lived. I've lied to myself for years. It's the only way I could stop from murdering myself. My own life was taken from me when I started working for The Devil and just because there's air in my lungs doesn't mean I'm alive. Hell, I'm more like the walking dead than anything else. I've always been worried about making it another day. In the process, I've failed to see my death clock has always been running. The Devil simply just adds minutes when he needs them. One day he won't. Shouldn't I live before then? Maybe I should run the clock out before he can. Is it bad I wanna run the clock out with Drew?

"Ouch!" I snap and quickly suck the blood from my pricked finger.

Stupid thorns. See? Mistakes.

Walking away to the opposite end of my greenhouse, I pass by my flourishing plants.

Unless you know a thing or two about plants, I wouldn't touch anything. There are quite a few things just lingering around that can kill you. You know why. You've seen why.

At my first aid station, I start to clean the prick, most people would've just brushed off.

Not in here. Can't risk that.

"Melody." Omar's voice echoes around my sanctuary.

"Over here!" I call back patting the spot dry before grabbing a band-aid.

His heavy footsteps make it easy to track him. Within seconds he's beside me. Frowning. "How'd you do that?"

"I caught it on a thorn."

"You rarely ever make that mistake."

"Thank you," I sarcastically remark. "I'm aware."

"How'd you do it?"

"It just happened."

He folds his arms across his chest with a displeased expression. "That doesn't just happen to someone who lives and breathes greenery. That's like saying 'my gun just went off'. That's not an acceptable excuse."

As soon as the bandage is around my finger I look up at him. "Did you actually need something from me or did you just come to accuse me, once more, of not being able to do my job?"

"Are you doing your job?"

"Wow." I snap. "How many times do I have to repeat myself?"

"What happened this morning?"

"Excuse me?"

"I checked in briefly this morning. I saw you walk into the bathroom. Audio seemed to cut out for a period of time. What happened?"

The memory of Drew's mouth consuming mine fervidly causes the unused muscles between my legs to clench like they did when it happened. "I gave him his medication and left."

"After telling him there weren't cameras in there. Why'd you do that?"

"What does it matter if he knows he's not being watched while he pees? What does it matter if he has that little bit of information, Omar? He's a dead man anyway you look at it, right?"

I wanna be wrong. I want Drew to be right. I want him to wrap me up in his arms and whisk me away like some trashy paperback novel. I want us to live a long and happy life together in a house with a backyard and a bunch of kids running around, but while I'm stupid enough to dream about it, I'm not stupid enough to buy it. He's going to die. He's gonna die and it's going to be my fault. Hate me. Go ahead. I do.

He hums.

"Why were you watching the feed anyway?"

"I told you. The way you look at him-"

"Hasn't stopped me from fulfilling my obligation."

"Yet."

"Which is what matters. I would appreciate a little respect. We may not trust anyone in this business, but I've at least earned that much respect from you all of people."

A brief hurt look crosses his face before he nods. Afterward he adjusts his jacket. "You need to pack an overnight bag. We're leaving."

Doing my best to hide my annoyance I question, "When?"

"After their call."

"Where?"

"Wherever The Devil wants us."

I roll my eyes. "What am I supposed to bring?"

"He wants a Truth Serum and a Mind Eraser. Two of each."

"Painful?"

"Extremely," he replies. "We are leaving immediately after the call. Do not linger."

"Who's going to keep an eye on Drew?"

"Drew?" Omar raises his eyebrows. "You mean McCoy."

I like his first name better, don't you?

"Yes."

His eyes glare, but he doesn't poke the subject. "He can fend for himself for two days. Melody-"

"He's not Jimmy," I whisper before he can start with the speech.

"He's not." Omar nods. Slowly he leans forward and growls, "He's worse. Do. Not. Forget. That."

He doesn't say anything else as he stomps out the way he came.

There's no way he can be worse than Jimmy unless he sets baby orphans on fire, which would be the only way I think of he could be worse. Is Drew messing with me? Is he using me as a pawn in a chess match with The Devil? I know. I know. I should be able to tell the difference and I thought I could until he kissed me. When he did that something inside of me snapped. Something I wasn't expecting. This is bad, isn't it? So very bad...

With my steel case now packed as requested, I head back into the main house where Drew is at the kitchen table, shirtless, clay clinging to him in such a fashion I'm hoping when he needs help scrubbing it off he asks me.

Oh God...what is wrong with me?

"You know when you blush you look even more beautiful," he mutters, eyes still on the terrible replica he's created. "Just saying..."

The redness to my cheeks deepens. I do my best to shoo it away. I grip the case tighter. "How's it coming along?"

"Well...this version looks less like a dick, so that's something," he claims with a crooked smile. Looking over at me he tilts his head at me. "How was Eden?"

I wiggle my bandaged finger at him. "Dangerous as always."

A look of concern crawls on his face as he rushes across the room at me. "Shit, you okay?"

"Just a prick."

"No need to name call me for caring," he playfully says. When I roll my eyes with a smile at his humor he lifts my hand. "You sure you're okay?"

My body shutters at the touch rendering me silent. I nod.

"Okay," he whispers softly, giving it a gentle stroke. His lips are slowly met by his tongue as he leans closer to me. Anticipating exactly what I want, exactly what I shouldn't want, I carelessly close my eyes and lean forward too. At that moment there's a ringing that seems to echo throughout the house.

"Right!" I snap and jump back. "Follow me."

"What is that?"

Informing him on our way to his bedroom, I state, "The video conference ring tone."

"Video conference?"

In a hushed tone, I explain, "You were only supposed to get one more call with Daniel before the event. I scored you another. Make it count, but remember it's being monitored."

Drew's jaw slips open. "You...you did that for me?"

Slowly I nod. "But if The Devil gets wind that this call wasn't necessary, the consequences will be astronomical. Be. Careful."

See? Stupid mistakes continue. The Devil didn't believe me when I told him that Drew needed the call. He's suspicious. Not as bad as Omar, but enough that I need to make sure nothing else happens between Drew and I. Call this my attempt at penance.

"Why?" Drew whispers. "Why did you risk this for me?"

"I know what it's like to miss your family and not be able to get to them. No one deserves that. Especially not you."

"I-"

"Melody says you need to speak to the other one," The Devil snaps on the screen a cigar dangling from his lips. "Why?"

"Sculpting your piece of shit art work is a bit harder than it looks," Drew growls back.

"So?" He tosses a hand in the air. "How would talking to your look a-like help?"

"He's more informative than he looks." When The Devil doesn't blink, Drew adds, "Or you can give me access to the outside world? The internet maybe?"

"So you can leave a trail for your computer genius brother to find you. I don't think so."

The Devil pushes a button and Daniel's face appears on the screen. His face looks like it's healing faster since I recommended

Nina treat with a special mixture I came up with myself, back in the early days to help Omar.

"Middle Man," Drew sighs, relief clear as day on his stressed face.

That. That right there. That glimmer of hope is what The Devil feeds on. And that small glimmer of hope is what Drew needed to stay alive in this hell. That's what he needs so he doesn't become the heartless harlot I am. His hope...his hope might just get him out alive. Well that and if I stop doing my job.

Daniel, drops the wrench and smiles in the camera. "Triple D!"

"You look...you look like you have all your limbs." Drew smirks. "Impressive."

"Right? For three days in this bitch. Yeah."

The Devil grunts. "Enough of the sentiments. Get. To. The. Point."

Drew asks, "Hey, you remember our Jimmy Neutron routine for art?"

Daniel looks confused for a brief moment, but then nods. "Yeah. Good old Jimmy Neutron."

"Was the trick to use a toaster oven or a hair dryer?"

"Hair dryer," he answers. "You want the flexibility. Just like a custom paint job. Always need not only the ability for an even color but an even dry."

Drew nods and The Devil snaps, "Is that it? Are you two finished?"

"Yeah," the two of them agree in unison.

"Good," he snaps. "Melody, I expect you out the door. McCoys, I expect my projects to be finished on time."

The screen goes black and Drew turns to me, knowing better than to smile or any other indicator that this was a bonus rather than a necessity.

Unhappy, Drew folds his arms across his chest. "You're leaving?"

"I have to."

"Be back for dinner?"

With a brief shake of my head, I turn to exit the room not giving him an exact time, since I'm not even sure myself.

"But you will be back, right?" The desperation in his voice, stops me in my tracks.

Looking at his brown eyes that are losing the small light of hope that was just returned to them, I give the smallest nod possible. My body turns around and heads for my room to grab my always packed overnight bag.

At least when the time comes and Drew sees me for what I am, he'll know that I did at least one kind hearted thing for him, even if it wasn't much.

Drew

Two days in this place alone haven't been fun. You don't realize just how much you hate solitude until it's not a choice. I haven't been completely alone. Two of the morons who helped kidnapped me are always on guard, but Melody hasn't been back. There hasn't been fresh breakfast made or any meals for that matter. The frozen meal bullshit reminds me of being at home when Knox isn't around. It makes me miss them even more than I already do. I can't wait to get the fuck out of here. Do you think Knox will mind sharing the kitchen with Mel? I don't. But isn't there a saying about too many cooks in the kitchen or some shit?

Groaning, I rub my calf where the bullet grazed me. The simple action shoots more pain through my body.

Why is my body so fucking stiff? And these aches don't seem to be fading. They only seem to be getting worse. It makes it difficult to work on shit when you feel like an 80 year old man. Melody's pain killers dulled whatever is wrong, but I haven't been given anything in her absence. I hope she returns home soon if not just to put the heartbeat back in this cell block, but to help make the other bodily pain go away as well. Two kinds of aggravation without her around.

Fuck, that's new too. Is this how normal people feel when they're...whatever it is I am, with her?

Through a grumble, I slide out of bed and head for the bathroom, each step more and more painful. As soon as I reach the bathroom, I grip the side of the counter top. Struggling to stay up right, I focus on the counter, eyes tempted to close. On a deep breath, I reach for my tooth brush, the aches pure agony.

"You look miserable," Melody's voice sweetly says.

Instantly I turn my face to see her leaning in the doorway with a glass of water and two tablets.

Knowing we're being recorded, I mouth, "That's what happens when I miss you."

She smiles brightly. "Take these. You'll feel better."

I motion my finger for her to come further into the bathroom. Instantly debate drags itself on her face. My mouth pleads without vocalizing the actual words, "Please."

Melody takes a few steps towards me, using the heel of her foot to nudge the door slightly closed. "Take these. Now."

"If I do, can I kiss you?" I mouth.

She stifles her smirk, but nods.

Without further hesitation, I take the pain killers, and two large gulps of water. As soon as I'm done, I wrap my hands around her hips and roughly press our lips together. A squeak comes out of her that I realize might raise suspicions.

I need her to make more sounds. I'm desperate to hear her moan. To hear her cry out for me.

Guiding her body to the bathroom closet door with one hand, I use the other one to start the shower in hopes it'll drown out most of the sounds. Fully embracing her with both my hands, I nip at her bottom lip for approval of my actions. When her tongue slips out to lightly tease mine, I groan and grind my hips against hers. Our tongues tangle as my hands slip under the waist band of her white scrubs. The second my fingers graze the outside of her underwear, a moan seeps out of her lips, pulling them away from me.

Greedy for more of those sounds, I latch my mouth onto her neck, sucking and nibbling while my fingers slide through the front of her panties to graze her clit. Melody's nails clamp down on my side.

A passionate growl comes from me. As quiet as I can, I command, "Open for me."

She spreads her legs, planting one on the side of the tub. Wasting no time, I glide two fingers inside of her, eliciting a sharp breath followed by a low cry of satisfaction. Before I can even relish the amazing sound, my name is sighed softly like a prayer. "Drew..."

Certain, I've never heard anything so beautiful in my entire life, I relocate my mouth to hers, devouring every taste I can find. With my fingers and tongue working as a team, I steadily steer her towards the pinnacle of ultimate pleasure.

Lost in the languorous laps our tongues seem to be engaged in, it doesn't register that she's managed to drop my sweat pants, until her warm hand is palming my cock. At that exact moment it's my lips that falter. "Fuck..."

My eyes struggle to open, to see hers fighting to do the same. We're both desperate to see the other one swimming laps in the pool of arousal that's trying to drown us. Melody's hand begins stroking in such a way it gives me the illusion she's afraid of hurting me.

Her delicate little hands couldn't hurt me if they fucking tried.

Seeing the need for encouragement she's seeking, I nod and brush our mouths lightly together, whispering against her mouth, "Keep going, baby."

Melody's tongue touches my top lip. Her hand increases in speed. Suddenly I'm so engrossed with the feeling of her hand working my shaft and toying with the piercing on my tip that my fingers start to slip from their original mission.

"So close," she announces, dragging my mind back to the mutual goal we're sharing. I smirk and glue our kisses back together. Our hands and bodies rock against one another in a rhythm I've never experienced before. Somehow every time she takes a pleasurable pump from me, she returns it tenfold. The gift of gratification then causes me to strive to give something even better, which just repeats the erotic cycle, the pending orgasm just breaths away.

Her body begins tensing and I know what's ahead. I know what's moments from presenting itself. Thankful since I'm only a pump away myself, I push her over the edge until her pussy is pulsating around my fingers while breath after breath is robbed from her to further flame the orgasm she's riding. If I wasn't about to come already, that sight would've done it. Letting go with her, I shower her fingers with warm streams, my face buried in her neck in an attempt to bury the bellowing roars.

Satiated, we're suddenly statues, stuck together in not only one solid stance, but one solid moment.

I've never experienced anything like that in my entire fucking life. There's getting off...and then there's whatever that was...I want more of that in my life. That's the kind of shit I want in it forever.

After a cold shower, alone, I wander into the kitchen where Melody is placing bagels and fresh fruit on the table. Warmly I greet her, the sight one I could easily spend the rest of my life getting used to, "Morning."

She greets back, "Morning. Feeling better?"

"I've never felt this fucking amazing in my life."

The compliment flushes her face and turns her away from me. "I bet you say that to all the girls."

"They say that to me."

My correction causes her to look at me again. "I can see why."

Pleased by the compliment, I drop down into the chair. "They won't get that chance again, though."

A subfuscous look appears on her face. "Why do you say that? I thought you planned to make it out of this alive?"

"I do." Resting my arms on the table, I watch her sit down beside me. "I meant, as far as I'm concerned, you're the only one from this point on I wanna make feel that way."

Melody giggles and hands me a napkin. "That's crazy."

I drop it in my lap and grab my bagel. "Why's that crazy?"

"Aside from the fact you just met me?"

Candidly I point out, "I met you five days ago."

"Still...that's...crazy fast to wanna...whatever it is you wanna with me. I mean, that is crazy right?"

Hey, my side. Don't go agreeing with her.

My tongue licks away the cream cheese from the corner of my lips. "Maybe for some."

"For most."

"Maybe." I shrug. "In all the years I've been around chicks, I've never once felt about them the way I do you. That means something to me. Just because it didn't follow some bullshit time line or some bullshit predictable scenario, doesn't make it any less real. My old man used to say 'When you know, you know.'. I used to think he was full of shit." A dreamy look appears in her blue eyes. "But he wasn't wrong. And he wasn't just talking about chicks. He meant for life. When you know, you know. The right job. The right car. The right life. It's a feeling once you get, you don't let go."

To my surprise, she slides her hand over under the table. "And you know?"

"I knew the minute you touched my face and promised the pain would fade. I just didn't know you meant more than what was in my leg."

My words seem to still her body. "What do you mean by that?"

"Merrick died at the hand of The Devil, just months ago-"

"I know," she cuts me off. "I um...I was the one who tended to his girlfriend while she was being held hostage."

"Jo?" An unusual feeling cuts me as I remember the longing they had for each other. The excruciating suffering they felt when they were ripped apart. "You took care of Jo?"

Merrick loved Jovi enough to give up his own life for hers. I feel like that's what a McCoy does. Dies to let something they love live. Mom died giving birth to Merrick. Merrick died trying to save the love of his life. Before you ask me is it worth dying for, I'm going to assume, you've never met something worth that kind of love.

"I did," she confesses. "She was...a sweetheart."

"Didn't get to spend much time around her, but she...she changed my baby brother. Couldn't fucking figure out why. They'd only been together weeks and it was like he was a completely different person. I used to wonder how meeting one person could do that to someone. The foundation you've stood on for your entire life should be sturdier than that...but dad was right. When you know, you know."

"He died in prison." She states in a way that causes my eyebrows to furrow. "Your father. It was...uh...it was in the McCoy file."

"Right." I clear my throat. "He died in prison. Mom died giving birth to baby bro. Madden spent most of his life raising us. What about you? You said your dad died of an overdose."

"He did. My mother worked two jobs to take care of me."

"And now?"

"When I first disappeared, she exhausted her efforts trying to find me. About six months in, The Devil informed me she took her own life."

Wanna bet he had her killed?

"Anyway, she worked a job cleaning offices at night and a secretary job during the day. Academic scholarships helped me through most of the school stuff. I had a couple little jobs to try to help, but most of my time was spent studying. I had my dream job all lined up for when I graduated..." The look of solemnness returns, but she tries to push past it before it settles. "What's it like being a triplet?"

Memories from all the trouble we've caused over the years makes me smile as I swallow the last of my bagel. "For the most part, pretty amazing."

"But?"

"But..." my voice trails off as my eyes meet hers. "But sometimes people don't take the time to care that you *aren't* the same person. They see you or they've heard about you and assume that you're all just alike. That it doesn't matter where one starts and where one ends. Girls line up to fuck you not because they find *you* irresistible, but because you're a carbon copy of the one they saw first. Sometimes...sometimes I wish I could be Drew instead of Triple D. Being a unit is...fucking incredible, but sometimes, being an individual is better."

Her hand squeezes mine and she whispers, "You'll always be Drew to me."

I smile softly and look down at the plate.

Are you starting to get it now? Why she's special? Why I can't leave this place without her? Could you walk away from the one person who sees you? The you that's hidden in the dark. The you that's not overshadowed by your job or your responsibilities. Could you walk away from the one person who risked their life to let you get a glimpse of the one you're missing? I can't. Fuck it. I won't. I don't give a fuck what you think.

Melody

Every time I'm around Drew I feel like I'm the old me. The person I was before I was hardened by a drug tyrant. Almost like the person I was before I met Jimmy, but better. Even better than that person, whoever she was. Why couldn't we have met under different circumstances? It's been seven days and I feel like we've been together a life time. How is that possible? Better yet, how much longer can I go on like this? Is it bad that it scares me more for Drew to find out the secret I'm holding, than it does for The Devil to find out?

"Come on Mel." Drew chuckles and shoves the end of his sandwich in his mouth. "You mean to tell me you never kicked around a soccer ball as a kid?"

"I'm not really good with balls."

He gives me a devious smirk.

Oh you shut it too!

"You do know this means we have to kick one, right?"

"We don't have one here."

Drew stretches out his legs and leans back on his palms, his amazingly tan, sculpted body looking like an ancient temple waiting to be worshipped at.

It can't be humanly possible to look that good all the time.

His legs wiggle back and forth in the grass. "Well, we are adding that to the list of shit we do when we escape this place and get home."

He says that often. Home. I'm not even sure what home is any more. I used to think it would be with my mom, wherever she was. With her gone, I guess it seems more like a mythical idea. Kind of like getting out of this place.

"That's becoming a very long list."

"Sex until we can't come any more is at the top," he announces.

I toss my crust at him and roll my eyes. "That's all you think about."

"Have you seen you?" Drew comments back, picking the crust up off his shirt. "You cannot blame me for that being constantly on my brain."

Watching him consume the last of my lunch, I pull knees to my chest. "I'm probably not even good at it."

"Why wouldn't you be good at it?" His eyes widen. "Are you-"

"No," I quickly spew. "Well...not technically."

His eyebrows lift. "Not technically?"

"I've had one boyfriend and we um...we did it once."

"Was he a little slower than the average bear? How could he get a taste of you and not attempt to overdose?"

My face starts to glow scarlet as I stutter, "I-I-I-"

"Beautiful."

On a huff I look down at my bare feet that are enjoying the cool grass. "We did it once and he said it was awful. When I suggested we could practice he..." my voice starts to fade remembering the expression of rejection on his face that was soon followed with disgust.

"Hey," Drew's voice whispers, his body now leaned closer to mine. When I don't look up, he uses the tip of his finger to turn my face to his. "He sounds like a fucking moron, but his mistake of letting you go, is one I'm grateful for. If it doesn't go well the first time, I have no qualms about practicing until it's perfect." Sensing a smile he adds, "And then continuing constant practice to keep it perfect."

I nudge him in the side, the playful motion causing him to laugh in victory.

There will probably never be a moment where that's a real possibility, but the false serenity of it is enough for me. I know The Devil feeds the soul hope. Problem is knowing and continuing to feast on it anyway.

Still laughing, Drew bumps his body into mine again. Now chuckling with him, I push back. The movement causes him to poke me in the ribs, a play fight ensuing. In a fit of giggles, the two of us start to wrestle in the grass. Rolling around, we take turns pinning the other down until the laughter makes it hard for anyone to win.

As we catch our breath, I watch the bird fly free across the sky, feeling my own taste of freedom for the first time. Abruptly I stand and dust off the grass covering my body. "Come on. Let me show you Eden."

Drew hops up, does the same, and follows me across the yard to the building that is almost the same size as the cottage itself. After I key in the code, I open the door exposing him to the only sanity that is constant in my world.

"Whoa..." he manages to whisper out only two steps in. "This is...remarkable."

Sheepishly I reply, "It's my sanctuary."

"I can see why," he mumbles and continues to stroll away from me, jaw still slightly agape.

"Just don't touch anything," I warn.

With a smug playful smirk he asks, "Afraid I'll break something?"

"More like, afraid it'll break you."

Before you're supposed to be broken...You don't touch anything either. I have enough death counts on my conscious.

"Concern for me," he pretends to be flattered. "My, oh my."

I roll my eyes and fold my arms across my chest. "More like concern that you deliver at least one more orgasm before you escape."

"The truth exposed." Drew chuckles and continues his casual walk passing the area dedicated to flowers. "And it's before *we* escape."

Humming, I simply follow behind him, answering questions that are rolling out of his mouth about the different colored plants he spots. The casual tour continues, information rushing out of me faster than I'm sure he can process, which doesn't surprise me. What I find shocking is the fact he continues to listen. That he continues to make an effort to care about what matters to me.

Jimmy never did.

By the time we're almost all the way back around, he sighs, "That's...this...fucking, wow. It's insane."

"A little," I coo.

"Who knew mother-nature could be such a bitch?"

The joke makes me smile wide. "She's as much a giver as she is a taker."

"I wouldn't mind a little giving and taking," his voice drops to a familiar tone.

My pussy dampens in response. When my mouth drops to respond, only a very quiet whimper comes from me.

Pleased, Drew smiles brightly. "Thanks for showing me this, Mel."

In an airy tone, I reply, "You're welcome."

He takes a deep breath and steps towards me, the tips of our fingers barely linked together. Preparing for the kiss, I start to shut my eyes, anticipating the overwhelming sensation that's soon to follow.

The sound of the green house door opening startles us apart. Rex's face appears around the corner. For a moment he just stares at the two of us, eyes oscillating back and forth.

Not appreciating the skeptical looks for simply standing so close together, I fold my arms across my chest. "What?"

His hands slide into his pockets. "What are you two doing in here?"

"I came to give him an idea of the portion of herb that would be needed to be stuffed inside the statue." I lie. "In other words, I'm doing my job. Why aren't you doing yours?"

"I am," he grunts in return. "There's a delivery for the prisoner."

"Delivery?" Drew questions.

"That's why I'm here." Rex snaps. "You honestly think I wanna spend more time around a McCoy than I have to?"

Sensing Drew's defensive nature coming, I brush past him. "Come on. I have a delivery for you to take back to Omar."

"There's a package for you too..." Rex sighs. "From The Devil."

A small twinge of terror tears it's way through me.

That's not good. No way is that good.

"I need you to take something back to Omar for me," I casually repeat, giving the illusion it's business as normal.

Anything less and I'm more fucked than I am now.

The three of us head back into the house where I spot Drew's small box on the table. He immediately goes to open it while I grab a small prepackaged requested chemical mixture from the fridge.

I offer it to Rex who is on my heels. "Straight to Omar. You have forty minutes or it's ruined. And if it's ruined, it's your ass not mine."

Rex smirks and snatches it from me. "Yeah, yeah, yeah." As I could've predicted, he smiles. "What do you say to dinner with me tonight? Get you out of this little box and some well-deserved time away from that asshole?"

There's an unmistakable growl from across the kitchen.

You heard it too right?

Just as Rex goes to snap at Drew, I inform him, "No. The answers always no, Rex. It's always been no. It'll always be no."

"But why?" he whines.

That's definitely one reason.

"1. You're not my type. 2. In this business, it's best not to get attached to anything or anyone." Hearing the words come out of me, hurts almost as much as knowing the truth behind them. I clear my throat to rid it of the anxiety. "Now, go. Clock is ticking."

Rex mutters something, but scurries out of the house.

Before Drew can ask me about what I said, I interfere. "What's in your package?"

"It's just Glycerin for fingerprints," he answers, eyes still on the tiny bottle in his hands. "There's a specific kind that's mixed with an unusual ingredient. Makes it easy to manipulate it the way necessary."

I hum and prepare to check my own delivery when his voice stops me.

"Is that really how you feel?" His eyes don't move from his hands. "You won't get attached to anyone?"

Unconsciously I answer, "It was true." The moment his eyes lift I add, "But things change."

The sight of his smile dismisses me from the kitchen to my bedroom, where the perfectly wrapped box with a bow is sitting on my bed.

Gifts from The Devil are never gifts. They're punishments. As far as real presents are concerned, I haven't received one since before I was trapped here.

Quietly I close my bedroom door before sitting on the edge of my mattress. On a deep exhale, I pull at the ribbon and remove the lid. My hand rushes to cover my mouth as I stare down at Jimmy's stiff finger that has a gaudy gold ring on it.

On the piece of white paper underneath the warning is short.

Choices Eve.

With my jaw trembling, I keep my hand clasped over my mouth to hold the sound inside.

His message is as loud and clear today as it was the first time I ever heard him say it. What am I supposed to do? Tell me...what am I supposed to do?

Drew

After showing me Eden, Melody disappeared into her room where she's stayed most of the afternoon. Not real sure if it was because she knew I had work to do or because of the package The Devil had delivered to her, so I simply let it go.

I have to keep up my end of the deal or there will be no escaping. No rescuing. Sometimes we have to take orders from someone we never fucking thought we would in order just to make it one more day. It's all good. I'm a McCoy. I'll survive. The Devil will get what's coming and lose one more ally on his side when I take her out of here with me.

While I'm thankful she wasn't around as I toyed with finger print making, I have missed her. Just her presence in the room seems to remind me that there is a light at the end of the tunnel. A sweet melody of hope to keep my mind from wandering towards the idea that I very well may die at the end of all of this.

With a melancholy expression on her face, Melody slips out of her room and into the kitchen. Freezing my body in place, I simply watch, curious what's bothering her. Desperation for her to confide in me grows.

I can't blame her for not. She's like watching a caterpillar who bloomed into a beautiful butterfly, all in captivity. Trapped with only her own beauty for so long. Seeing the outside world with all it's splendor and evil revolve around her, all in hope of the lid coming off. Well we're taking that lid off. We're freeing that butterfly. Soon...very soon.

She tries to put on a smile. "Hungry?"

Closing up the last of my materials that don't need to sit out to dry, I shrug. "I could eat." Hopeful I offer, "Want me to cook?"

She shoves a hand on her hip. "You can cook?"

"Define cook," I tease, which makes her roll her eyes, a hint of a smile appearing. "I mean I can boil water."

"That's a start," Melody replies opening the fridge.

"I can then add the noodles to it." My playfulness continues as I cross over to her. "I can also stir, drain, and add the cheese sauce making a gourmet dish."

A giggle reluctantly gets away. She shakes her head and looks over her shoulder at me. "Macaroni and cheese. You can make mac and cheese."

"I am the reason you get the blue box blues. It's just that great when I make it." My fingers lightly touch her arm. The simple action seems to cause her to jump out of her skin and right into my arms. Concerned by her jitteriness I whisper, "Everything okay?"

"Fine," she lies.

It's that obvious. Hell you can see it too.

"Please don't lie to me," I beg in a hushed tone.

Her eyes gloss over. "Please, don't make me talk about it."

I give her a slow nod of understanding. "Dinner?"

"Dinner."

Reaching around her, I open the fridge once more to peer inside. "Hm...is that...is that steak? We can have steak?"

"That's more for your last night here."

I joke, "Like a last meal?" When sadness seeps back into her expression, I divert, "What about mac and cheese?"

"You're serious?" She wipes away a tear that's somehow made it's way to her eyes. "You want macaroni and cheese out a box?"

"Don't knock it before you try it."

Melody sniffles. "I don't think I have any."

"Do you have noodles?"

"Yeah."

"Milk? Cheese?" She nods. "Whatever it is that makes stuff turn to sauce?"

"Flour?"

"Yes." I point. "Failed home ec forgetting that shit."

Almost as if she's impressed, she leans against the counter and looks up at me, eyes shimmering. "You took home ec?"

"Yes."

"Why?"

"Any idea how easy it is pick up chicks when you're one of three dudes in that class? Not to mention the hottest?"

Grinning she starts to chortle. "You are unbelievable..."

"I always hoped you'd say that in different circumstances, but for now, I'll take what I can get." When her eyes flash the passion I'm anxious to see more of, I sigh, willing my hard on away. "Let's make some mac and cheese..."

"Let's do it."

A lesson to the wise. Do not pop a hard on near an open flame. Burning the tip of your dick is a fucked up thing to have to learn the hard way. Just...take my advice. With that said, don't do something to make your husband or boyfriend pop one while he's boiling water. That's fucked up...

Melody and I work together to make the dish from scratch. She explains cooking fundamentals.

Like why the pasta I felt was done, wasn't actually done. It just would've been a little extra hard. Who's ever complained about an added crunch?

While she stirs the noodles, observing them like a child that needs constant supervision, I grate the cheese, snacking between bites even when she fusses at me not too. Annoyed by my eating she abandons her post to pop me on the hand. As soon as she does, I grab her fingers, angle us so our backs are hidden to the camera and bring her fingers to my lips kissing each individual one. The sweet notion isn't lost. In fact it's rewarded with soft purrs and innocent whimpers.

Melody slides away from me to return to her task. Eventually, we combine everything, create the sauce between playful kitchen duels, and toss it in the oven creating more of a pasta bake than boring mac and cheese.

For the record, nothing wrong with boring mac and cheese. It is the perfect solution when all your favorite fast food joints are closed at 3 a.m. And you need post sex sustenance.

While waiting for it to finish cooking, Melody hops her body up on the counter. Unable to stay away like some sort of bug to a bright light I know could be my demise, I move myself to her. Standing between her spread legs, I gently stroke her calves.

I know I shouldn't, but I love touching her. Her skin is soft and sensual. Flawless.

With her eyes lingering in mine she asks, "What do you miss most besides your family?"

There's no hesitating. "Bertha."

"Bertha?"

I nod.

"Is that...Is that a girl you slept with regularly?"

Chuckling I help fleeting tension by continuing to rub her lovingly. "Bertha's my bike."

"Your motorcycle?" When I nod she lifts her eyebrows. "You named her Bertha?"

"Don't judge..."

You either.

Melody covers her giggles with her cupped hands.

"Bertha is a beast," I explain. "She's been my old lady for a while. Daniel, Destin, and I got matching bikes at the same time. Spent late nights customizing them so they were perfect fits."

"How'd you pick the name Bertha?"

I give her a short shoulder shrug. "She spoke to me. Gave her one look when I was finished and I heard a voice in my head say Bertha."

Melody giggles harder. "That's pretty funny."

"Bertha can handle some of the craziest tricks. Always cradles me perfect when I stand on her."

Shock shoots out of her. "You stand on her?"

"Oh yeah," I casually inform. "Stand. Pop wheelies. Burn outs. Some crazy shit you wouldn't even believe me if I told you. I don't do it much anymore, that's more Daniel's scene, but I *can* and Bertha takes good care of me when I do."

"That's insane..."

"Tell me something about being a McCoy that isn't?"

She smiles sweetly.

"What about you?" I redirect the question. "What do you miss?"

Her finger slips into her mouth.

Can my dick switch places with it?

Casually I adjust my crotch.

"Holidays."

"Holidays?"

"Yeah. They were one of the only times in my house where I really got to spend time with my mom. Most places were closed or gave her the day off, so they didn't have to pay her time and half. We'd bake cookies for the occasion. Cuddle on the couch. Drink milk and eat them while watching a holiday special. It wasn't ever anything extravagant. When my dad over dosed, his side of the family alienated us. Some blamed my mom. Some blamed me-"

"You were just a kid."

"I was 'too much' work for him." Her fingers roll around the end of her braid. "Anyway, my mom was an only child, my grandparents were in Canada. Outside of Christmas they rarely spoke. We couldn't afford to go see them, so...we made due with just the two of us."

Offering her a faint smile I say, "If it makes you feel any better when I was little there were tons of us and never enough presents."

She sighs, "It wasn't about the presents. It was about having family. I wished for a bigger family, but made due with what I had. I guess, I don't miss holidays themselves as much as family."

I press both my hands on the counter, one on each side of her legs. "With me, I promise you'll always have family."

Melody fights against her instinct to deny. "Promise?"

"Promise," I repeat. "They're loud. Pushy. Obnoxious as fuck sometimes. Invasive. But they're loving. And they'll learn to love you just like I'm learning too."

Panic soars into her eyes.

Oh no. Shit! Shit! Shit! Is there some sort of I love you rule? Why are you laughing at me? Do I look like I know this shit? I haven't even been on a date that didn't end in sex in...you know what? Never mind. Ignore that. How bad did I just screw this up?

The oven timer dings and grabs our attention. Taking a couple steps back, I move out of her way. Tempted to say something else, I rub my mouth instead, preventing my foot from further going into it.

She pulls out the dish and allows it time to cool while settling the plates with the fresh cut cucumber, tomato, and feta cheese salad she made.

It's not that Knox doesn't cook shit for us that's impressive, it's just impressive in a different way. More like a mass production sort of way. When you're feeding six boys...eventually six men, it becomes more about mass quantity first, high quality second.

I insist on filling the water glasses while she carries our food to the patio area where the cameras are easier to hide from.

Even left my mess all over the table to insure we could have some alone time. Crafty I know. Remember that when it comes time to escape.

As soon as both glasses are filled, I prepare to transfer them both when I notice the veins under my tatted wrist seem bluer than normal. Unsure if that's just a side reaction to the pain killers that are working miracles on my muscles or if something else is wrong, I let it roll off and rush off to my date.

That's right. It's now a date. A romantic picnic under the stars. Whoever said you can't date while being kidnapped, obviously has never met a McCoy.

On the patio floor, I set the glasses down on top of the blanket. Once I'm settled beside her, I wrap one arm around her lower back. She leans into my embrace.

Out here is almost as safe as the bathroom.

The two of us eat in silence for a few moments, the night singing praises for it's arrival from various creatures. While I know it's wrong to enjoy so much of this moment in which I'm supposed to be fearing for my life, I let it happen anyway. I soak up everything I can about Melody. I stain it all to memory.

"Drew," her voice meekly calls to me.

Just the sound of her lips letting my name slip out has my dick rising to the occasion. "Yeah, baby?"

"What if this is all we get?"

Bemused by the question, I ask, "What?"

"What if *this* is all we get? What if we don't get to escape? What if we don't get to finish that never ending list of things you want us to do together? What if all we get are these few moments in this house, in the middle of fucking nowhere?" Suddenly her blue eyes look up innocently. "Can that be enough for you?"

The question seems loaded. There seems to be one little fact, she's not telling me that I can't put my finger on. I want to push. I want to know what it is. The more information she can give me, the better more accurate of an escape I can make.

Desperation covers her words. "I need that to be enough for you."

"Melody!" A booming voice that is starting to make me hate more than before spreads through the house. "Melody!"

Flustered, she stands with her plate just as the door slides open. "Why are you yelling?"

"Why are you eating outside?"

She nonchalantly points. "You see the kitchen table?"

Omar glares at me before he looks back at her. "The living room is broken?"

"I don't like vacuuming any more than you do." By the expression on his face, he buys her reasoning. "Fair. I need a favor."

"*You* need a favor?"

Keeping my back turned to them, as if I'm not listening, I pick up my dishes.

"Yeah. I uh....have a medical condition I need a fix for."

"Your rash is back," Melody announces.

He grumbles, "Yeah. It's worse than before."

"I told you to stop sleeping with her," she scolds. "Her pussy is going to kill you."

My teeth clamp down on my tongue.

That gives an entirely different meaning to killer pussy. You're laughing too, huh? I see that smirk.

"Why aren't you using EA?"

"Don't...don't do that," Omar snaps. "Just fix me."

Lifting my dishes I announce, "I'm gonna wash these."

"Just leave 'em," Mel insists. "I'll wash 'em."

"You sure?"

"Yeah." She tugs at her braid. "Go ahead and rest or shower..."

"Yeah you've got clay by your eyebrows," Omar adds.

Told you I fucking hate clay.

I nod and stroll past them dropping my dishes in the sink. My eyes give Melody one more glance before heading for my room on the opposite side of the house.

No. These moments aren't enough for me and I know they aren't enough for her, but fear is a motherfucker. Especially if that's all you've known for so long. Soon enough she'll see there's nothing to fear. Soon she'll see The Devil on his knees before he's executed.

Melody

Lying in bed, I continue to stare up at the dark ceiling.

I can't do it. I can not sneak across the house and into bed with him. That's a terrible idea! It's beyond terrible! It's...it's...it's whatever is beyond terrible.

In another attempt to fall asleep, I close my eyes, visions of shirtless Drew parading across my eyelids. I want to battle the images almost as much as I want more of them. The image drops his pants revealing to me the long stiff member with a pierced crown I peaked at days ago. Helplessly I whimper while my pussy tightens, eager to feel him. Eager to feel that barbell rub inside me.

Have you ever felt anything like that before? I just had it in my hand and it was wonderful.

My eyes pop open as my hands start trying to crawl underneath my panties. Shocked by my own behavior I shoot straight up in the bed. I ruffle my hair in an attempt to wash the thoughts away. Wavering between wrong and worse, I stare out my bedroom window at the empty road that's rarely traveled by anyone outside of The Devil's associates.

He's gonna kill me. I already know that. The stupid finger in the box was just a heads up. Toying with his food before he eats it. He's sealed my fate and now it's a waiting game. If you knew you were gonna die, what would you do? Would you sit back and let your last chance at something more than the pathetic prison lifestyle you've become accustomed to slip away, or would you make every one of those moments you could count? Hm. You're right. Why are we still talking about this?

Slowly I slide out of bed, shed my clothes and slink across the pitch black house. Knowing exactly where the cameras are, I slither around most of the angles and right into Drew's room like this is an everyday occurrence.

It's not! First time I swear!

Inside I'm grateful the clock beside the bed illuminates the room just enough for basic help, but not enough to help the cameras. Very carefully, I peal back the blanket and crawl on top of him.

It doesn't take longer than a breath for him to stir and snap, "What the-"

My hand flies over his mouth. "Shhhh." There's a muffled objection, but he stills himself. In a quiet tone I whisper, "It's just me."

When I remove my hand he sighs, "Mel?"

I spread my bare thighs wider, the feeling of his skin against mine exhilarating. "Yeah."

His shaky voice asks, "Wh-what are you doing here?"

"Really?" I snap. "What do you think? This is an accident?"

"I am praying to God this isn't an accident or a mistake or a fucking dream," he grumbles, his hands now kneading my ass gently.

In an unsteady voice, I confirm, "It's not a dream."

Wishing I could make out his face even more, but thankful he can't make out mine to see my pending nerves, I run my hand down his chest. Drew shudders in response and grips me tighter.

"What about the cameras?" The tone in his voice sounds strangled. "What if-"

"As long as I'm gone before morning, we should fine. The cameras are shitty at night. The light from the clock barely registers."

Before he can ask any more questions, my mouth falls on top of his. Instantly Drew groans something fierce and tugs my body up, his pierced tip nudging, teasing my clit. The sensation immediately pulls our mouths apart so I can let out a soft moan of passion.

"Fuck..." Drew responds. His dick twitches. "Baby...I don't think I can wait any longer."

"Please don't." I beg. "Just...just go slow, okay?"

"Promise," he answers before using his hand to shift his dick to my entrance. The ring acts as a warning of the pleasure that's to come. My body shakes in anticipation, a moan coming out of me already. Drew lets out a slow sigh, "Keep that shit up and sex with me is gonna look like a bad joke."

Unsure of what he means, I ask, "I don't...I don't-"

"Mel, I'm already holding back to the point I'm afraid I'm gonna break my dick, but if you keep moaning and shuddering like that, this is gonna be over before I even get started."

Did you know what he meant? I've never...never had this kind of problem before.

My giggling makes him grumble, "Not exactly a laughing matter..."

I roll my eyes and brace myself. Slowly Drew's cock pushes inside, the girth tearing the un-stretched muscles to the point of pain. My body tenses. I whimper.

"Relax," Drew whispers, his hands stroking my back. He pulls my chest so it's flush with his. Tightly his arms flex around my body caging me. My face falls into the crook of his neck. "I'll take care of you, Mel. Just let me."

His cock draws back before pushing in again. This time my muscles seem to be more willing to accommodate the intrusion. Drew repeats the action, the steady space, exactly what my body wants by the way my pussy starts soaking.

"Fuck..." Drew groans again, his lips beside my ear. "Your body is Heaven baby and I never wanna leave." My tongue softly darts out to taste the skin on his neck. He whimpers and begs, "More..."

I lick again just as his piercing hits a spot that forces me to hiss loudly.

He flexes his arms around me and rocks against the destination once more. "You like that?"

Instantly my pussy clenches and I shudder out another moan, the building pressure unfamiliar and teetering on overwhelming. Instead of reading the signs as a reason to stop or change position, he thrusts harder. Sharper. He hits the spots with perfect precision proving his devotion to providing pleasure. My breathing becomes harsh while my body struggles to understand the building explosion that's pending. I've felt it once before with him. I want to feel it again.

"Drew," I meekly plead.

"You need to come," he insists robbing my mouth of the remaining part of that sentence. "I need you to come..." His request has my hips moving to match his movements. "I need to feel that again."

Without waiting for further invitation my orgasm violently rips through, clamping down on his cock so hard I'm convinced I'm going to bruise it.

I don't think that's possible...but I'm just gonna ask for reassurance here. That's not a thing right?

As my voice softly sings my body's new found devotion in rounds, his body goes rigid, the grip around me so suffocating, I'm not sure if I'll ever breathe again. An animalistic growling comes out of him at the same time a warm rush fills my pussy igniting the orgasm that was fading to combust once more. The undulating blaze of our climax continues until our bodies collapse in an overheated heap.

Holy shit....is that what sex is supposed to be like? Why did I have to wait until I was a dead woman walking to discover that?

Drew

On a yawn I scratch my bare chest, the simple action excruciatingly painful. Unsure if it's from the best sex I've ever had or from whatever seems to be bothering me every morning, I simply stay still a moment longer.

Look, this is gonna make me sound like a giant pussy. I'm aware. But fuck. Whatever that shit was last night, had to be more than sex. I've had a lot of sex. I've had enough sex to last some people lifetimes. Yes. Multiple lifetimes. Up until last night I prided myself in the legend of the McCoy reputation reigning true. Truth is what happened last night, wasn't because I know what the fuck I'm doing. No. That was because of both of us. I need to do that again. Hell, I need to do that shit for the rest of my life. Did I tell you I almost busted a nut twice in one session? That's not even humanly possible. Or is it?

I struggle to raise my body up knowing I need to rinse the smell of Mel away.

Not that I fucking want too. She smells like fresh flowers and oranges. A sweetness that matches her personality. Besides, her pussy loved my cock so much it painted it with five orgasms in the couple of hours we were together. You're damn right I fucking counted.

On my way to the bathroom, I try to stifle the urges to wince. Uncertain that the shaking isn't from an invading infection, I stop and check myself out as best as I can. My veins still look a little blue on my wrists. It could be from the lack of sun I've been getting. It could be nothing more than sun withdrawal.

You know, winter color setting in early.

Looking down I begin searching for other discolorations when my vision blurs.

What the fuck?

I rub my eyes and everything looks clear again. Certain I just need a shower, I grit my teeth through the discomfort and get my shower started. Warm water washes away the evidence that Melody gave herself to me as well as the lingering clay bits, which are proof of my actual purpose here.

"Morning," Melody's voice echoes in the bathroom.

With a smirk, I pull the corner of the shower curtain back immediately noticing the way the door is slightly shut behind her. "Morning."

"Take these," she routinely instructs holding out the glass of water and tablets for me.

"Fine," I reply in an attempt to sound like our routine.

We have to keep up appearances in the light, even if we get to fuck in the dark.

While ingesting the medication, I can't help but watch her watch me. Her mouth is slightly unhinged, her tongue seems to be outlining my abs on her lips, and her knees seem to be growing in desire to drop.

Fuck. Me. That's hot.

"Here." Offering her the glass back, I pull the curtain back, and nudge the shower head to hit tile instead of accidentally wetting her. "Anything else?"

Melody places the glass on the counter and states, "Breakfast will be served soon."

"Fine."

"Fine."

She drops to her knees, her hot mouth engulfing my stiff dick.

I bite my fist to stop the sharp groan from escaping. Knowing I need an exit line, but unsure of how it's gonna sound I sigh, "You can...you can go now." In hopes that is good enough to sound like a conversation ender, I thread my fingers through the back of her braided hair allowing my cock to slide further down her throat. Her tongue moves in waves on the underside of my shaft as her mouth sucks, determined to eventually taste my soul or whatever else she can squeeze out. Melody's mouth bobs on my cock silently, her tongue at times toying with the sensitive tip that's trickling pre cum in a way that feels like I'm already busting a nut. She explores, adventures down to my nuts several times before returning to sucking on my cock, the entire time tugging me to the brink of coming. Finally unable to hold out any longer, I tug at her hair, my body tenses as it tries to pull out before it can fill her mouth. Instead of pulling back, she prepares to receive her reward with the quietest hum. The vibration shuts my eyes while my body pours come out of me and into her relentlessly. Shaking through the ecstasy, I grip her hair for aid in my battle of buckling knees.

Melody's jaw frees my dick and I stumble back against in the tile right into the cold water.

Fuck it. I don't even care.

With the pleased grin of the little minx she is, she wipes the corner of her lips, grabs the glass and exits the bathroom leaving more than just my body empty.

Something seriously has to be wrong with me if I can't handle being away from her just a minute right?

After scrubbing down and dressing, I head for the kitchen where I see Mel with her back to me mixing two bowls of something. Curious I ask, "Eggs?"

"Parfaits," she corrects.

"What the fuck is a parfait?"

Don't laugh. Is there pork in it?

"It's yogurt, granola, and fruit."

"That's not breakfast. That's a snack."

"It's a healthy breakfast," she insists turning around to look at me. Slamming a hand on her hip she snips, "Since when do you get lippy about what you get fed?"

I wink. "Since I can't get my lips on other things."

Her rubricating cheeks makes me smile proudly. Melody shakes her head. "You are something else."

"So are you."

The compliment gets her to hum before she shoves the bowl my direction. "Eat up. You're running late this morning."

"I slept *really* well last night," I answer before shoving a mouth full of the disaster into my mouth. After just a few chews, I nod. "Not too bad."

Melody offers me a smile and has a bite of her own. The two of us start our standing breakfast rather than waste time trying to clear the table I'm going to be occupying in a short time anyway.

Seeing the sight of my materials drying on the table spurs my mind a direction.

"What was the present from The Devil yesterday?"

Her chewing ceases. "Why?"

"Because I asked."

With a quick shake of the head, she denies, "It's not important."

"Mel-"

"Drop it," she cuts me off.

"Mel-"

"I said drop it." Her bowl slams on the counter beside her. "The message he wanted me to receive came in loud and clear. It's in the trash now. Let's leave the subject with it."

Not thrilled at having to let the topic go, but thankful I got information I can use, I agree. "Fine." I have another bite before pushing another issue. "Can I ask a question about something else?"

She folds her arms across her chest, an annoyed glow in her blue eyes.

I know. I know. Not ideal post getting head conversation, but in order to get to more sex outside of this little cell in the middle of hell, I have to make some plans. I have to push some buttons. Wouldn't you to save the person you lov-. We're not gonna talk about that right now.

"Omar," I start.

"What about him?"

"Do you trust him?"

"No more than I trust anyone else in this business."

Trying not to take offense to that, I ask, "You two seem close."

"Really? Are you implying I'm sleeping with him?"

"Fuck no," my mouth spews, dropping the spoon in the bowl. "Well. Wait. Are you?"

The redness flashing on her face is not nearly as captivating as it is when she blushes.

Shit!

"Are you fucking kidding?"

"That's...that's not what I was trying to imply. I was just-"

"What were you trying to imply, Drew?'

"Do you care about him?"

Uncomfortable by the question, she fidgets with her braid. "I mean...yeah. He's looked out for me almost since day one."

Not surprised since it was what I was suspecting, I return to my breakfast.

"But I'm not an idiot." The addition to her answer lifts my face back up. "I know he wouldn't hesitate to sell me out if necessary. Especially if it meant to save his own skin." With a hard look she says, "We live in a world where it's kill or be killed. Don't doubt that."

That's just the thing. I don't.

Changing conversation, I use my spoon to point at the sculpture on the table. "What do you think?"

Mel glances at the sight and shakes her head. "Not quite."

Disappointed I grunt, "Really?"

"Well look here." She strolls over. "See these cracks here and here. They aren't on the actual sculpture. Someone who's been studying it for years would notice." Melody points to a lower spot, "The way it dried down here, indicates an added heat source. It's too smooth. Too perfect. It's a fairly aged sculpture, so the drying is most likely not going to be even because it was sun dried."

I put my bowl beside hers. "You know an awful lot about forgeries."

"I've seen enough of them done and fucked up," she sighs. "Oh. And you're hollowing technique is too obvious. One hit on the wrong spot and it's going to crumble."

"That's not-"

She taps the center and the sculpture shatters.

"Damnit."

Melody giggles briefly before the smile is wiped away. She greets, "Morning Omar."

"Melody," he states back. He gives me a harsh sneer before saying, "Got you more clay."

"Thanks," I reply reaching for the bag that's dangling from his fingertips.

"How the hell are you going through this shit so fast? You making molds of your dick or something?"

With a charming smile I answer, "Not since the first day."

Melody hides her giggle behind her hand. Omar immediately gives her a sharp scowl, which is when she snaps, "Oh lighten up. That was pretty good."

He grunts and shakes his head. "I have some appointments this morning, but I will be back to pick up the delivery."

"When?" she asks.

"When I'm done." Omar lifts an eyebrow. "Is that a problem?"

"It's a complicated order, Omar. I need a time estimate to insure that it is ready."

"You should have no problem if that is the only thing you are doing," he sternly states giving me another glare.

I really hate this guy. Have I mentioned that?

"There are other responsibilities-"

"Cooking for the *hostage* is not one," he growls. "Just in case you've forgotten that's what he is. Not a guest."

Melody press her lips together momentarily. "There are other responsibilities that require action now in order to be used later. This is not the only delivery The Devil has me filling in a timely fashion, so I will ask you again. When?"

Omar shoves his hands in his pockets. "This evening. Before dinner. You have been asked to escort the package as well."

She whispers, "Shocking."

"Wear something nice." Surprised by his words both of us lift our eyebrows. "The Devil has requested you as his date."

I fight the urge to lunge at him about it.

No good in whooping the shit out of the messenger just yet. Don't get me wrong. It's on the fucking to do list too.

"Fine." She nods. "I'll be ready."

Omar turns around and strolls out the way he came. The second the door shuts, I look at her and whisper, "Date?"

Mel denies, "It's not what you think."

Anger rises in my tone. "I think The Devil is changing your job description...are you gonna...are you gonna sleep with him?"

"Why is that the only thing your brain can come up with?" she snaps.

First instinct. Is that wrong? I don't want anyone touching my girl but me. Especially not that fuck.

"I'm not in the 'fuck him' division of his operations. If he wants me there, it's because he plans to poison someone and wants me to watch. He does this occasionally to remind me of my place in his world."

Seeing the anguish and trepidation in her eyes, I quickly try to apologize. "Mel I'm-"

"Don't." She raises her hand. "Just, shut up and follow me."

I do as I'm told. We make our way back into my room where she turns on the television screen. Unexpectedly there's a sight on it that brings a bit of relief to my system.

"Triple D," Madden sighs his own reprieve obvious. "You're both alive...You got all your limbs?"

With a small smirk I raise my fingers. "Ten fingers. Ten toes. One large and still functional cock." There's a squeak from behind me, which makes me smile brighter. "Yeah I'm alive."

"Daniel said he'd send us a tune," Madden announces the code. "Jackass has the nerve to joke about Bon Jovi at a time like this."

Clever. When we were first trying to avoid cops, we made sure we had code phrases we could drop that wouldn't raise suspicions. Things about music. Movies. T.V. Shows. Way of communicating between the lines. Daniel basically promised to send him a GPS signal the moment he could. My guess? The night of the heist. We're smarter than we look and always planning to escape less than pleasant situations.

I try not to smile. "What about you two? Surviving?"

"Barely," Destin whispers as he shakes his head. "The Devil is fucking us hard. Between spending most the day justifying all our spending to some dickhead auditors and spending most of the night searching for you two, I haven't slept. I forget to eat until Knox shoves a plate of food in front of my face."

Quickly noticing our female McCoy missing, I tilt my head. "Where is Knox?"

"Dealing with *actual* customers," Madden informs. "And I'm trying to deal with actual mechanic work. At this rate the shop won't stay open very long."

"Which is what The Devil wants," I sigh. "Don't worry. We'll be home soon."

"That's what Daniel said," Madden informs. "You better be. And your asses better be in one piece or when I glue you back together, I'm gonna rip you apart again."

He's loving in his own way. Just...go with it.

I chuckle. "Noted."

"Who's the chick?" Destin acknowledges.

"That's Mel," I quietly answer before turning around to give her a smile. She tries to hide the soft one she's developing. "She kinda likes me." When she rolls her eyes I turn back around to see a scowl on my big brothers face.

Him and Omar sure have that look fucking patented.

"Drew..." Madden warns.

"We're gonna save her too."

Destin slowly questions, "We are?"

"Yup." I answer and watch Madden's jaw twitch even though he doesn't say anything. "She's trapped just as much as I am in this place. She's been...good to me."

Fucking amazing, but they don't need to know that. I damn sure ain't sharing once she's out of here and I would hate for either of them to get that idea for even a second.

"How is it even while you're kidnapped, you and Daniel still get your dicks touched?" Destin complains. "I'm losing sleep trying to fucking find you. You're losing sleep trying to fucking find pussy."

"Don't talk about her that way," I snap, which stiffens both of them. "It's not like that. And that's the only time I'm gonna warn you."

Destin surrenders his hands, which is when Madden sighs, "I know that look."

That's because Merrick had it. Back then I thought it was a terrible thing to have. Now? Now I know it's worth every bit of shit he stirred up to keep it.

Leaning into the camera he grouses, "If you swing at me, I will not hesitate to lay your ass out."

The memory of Merrick throwing a punch at him over Jovi causes me to smile and nod. "Fair." After a brief pause I add, "Just don't give me a reason to."

There's a buzzing sound from behind me. In a calm voice, Melody says, "Say goodbye."

"I'll see you in a few days," I say with a wave.

The two of them offer me the best nods of solace they can before the screen goes black.

Turning around to face Melody, I'm surprised by the livid expression that's returned to her face. In a low tone she says, "I don't appreciate how one minute you can say shit like that and treat me like you do, think I'm not like every other female you've ever met, only to do a 180 and constantly wonder am I sleeping with everyone around me. When I told you I had been with one other person it wasn't so you would take pity and screw me. It wasn't a lie to make you feel special if we ever fell into bed together. It was one of the most truthful, more embarrassing things I've ever had to admit out loud. So make up your mind on which side of the equation you want me to sit on, Drew. Am I really someone you think is worth a damn or am I just like everything else that keeps crossing your path, disposable?"

Not shocked by the content of her speech, so much as the fact she made it, my mouth twitches to respond.

"I have work to do. If you need something, I'll be in Eden."

Melody spins on her heels and turns away without a second glance.

Was it that out of line to even let that cross my mind? In a world like this can you blame me for being curious every now and again if the sweet routine is an act? I don't think it is. I don't want it to be. When we're together, she feels like she would welcome an escape at the drop of a dime, but she's just given up. Then I look at her and see the way Omar says shit without saying it and can't help, but wonder what's the other side she's hiding? I know it's there. I ignore it the best I can. But I'm not a complete idiot no matter how blind love can make me.

Melody

With another heavy sigh, I scoop the powders together, the assignation mixture, not one of the easier creations I've come up with.

It's time consuming not just loving these plants, watering, them and insuring they grow properly without killing each other or me, but chemically stripping them into the different healing purposes and death functions The Devil desires. Sometimes I think he considers himself God instead of Satan.

I seal the small zip loc bag before wiping off the outside of it. Once any excess residue is removed, I tuck it in the brief case beside the other two mixtures that were requested of me.

All properly labeled. Don't worry.

As I pull off my latex gloves I hear the sound of my door opening across the greenhouse. Curious if Omar returned early I peer around to see Drew with a hurt expression on his face.

It's like looking at a wounded puppy. Ugh. Okay, so I snapped earlier. Maybe a little too harshly considering the fact I know he shouldn't trust me, but it hurts. It hurt to kind of let someone in, to risk your life for them, yet still have them assume every time your turn your back you may or may not be fucking the enemy. Which I'm not. I may be doing my job, less and less well every day, but I'm not screwing The Devil in the aspect recently implied.

Drew sighs, steps away from me. "I'm sorry."

His brown eyes begin to melt my will to stay strong. To keep the guard I just put back up. "Apology accepted." I turn around and close the briefcase. "I need to shower and change, but if you're hungry-"

His lips brush the side of my neck. "I am. For you." When my breath hitches he states, "You're the only thing I've been craving every minute since I've been here." A long lick slides up my neck. "And you're the only thing keeping me alive."

Oh...oh how wrong he is there. In fact...I'm the very thing killing us both.

Guilt rises in my throat, but is washed away by a warm kiss close to my ear. "Cameras. Where?"

"Th-there's one by the entrance and one..." my voice trails off at the feeling of his hands caressing my hips and ass. "In the opposite corner."

"Where can we not be seen?"

Glancing over my shoulder, I let our eyes meet. "There's a spot by the first aid station."

His eyes that are swarming with desire scream louder than his voice ever could. "Go. There. Now."

I nod and casually stroll away from him, past my work station, past the rows of plants mainly used for healing, to the small area I built for tending to the wounds I could receive while I'm in here. The second I reach the destination Drew's body is pressed against my back. Bracing myself I plant my hands firmly on the table.

The heat from his body almost scorches my own flesh that seems to be burning. In a whisper he asks, "How long do I have you to myself?"

"Not long," I whisper back, head falling forward at the feeling of my pants being dragged down.

"Then I'll make it count," he declares. Drew's palm pushes me forward, so my chest is against the table before he helps my lower half out of my scrub bottoms. Growling, he runs a finger down the back side of my pussy. "You don't wear underwear with your scrubs?"

Panting from the simple touch I answer, "Not usually."

His hot breath is against the area that can't wait a second longer to experience what it's like to have a tongue on it. "When we escape...you keep that fucking habit. Got it?"

"Got it." My compliance is rewarded with his mouth clasping onto the stickiness I've already created and allowing my juices to seep into his mouth instead of on my legs. "Oh my God..."

Drew hums his approval, whether it's of my taste or my response is unknown, and begins to consume the craving he claimed he had. Mercilessly his tongue rolls around, presses against my clit, turns and twists until my knees wobble. My cries of his name are quiet not because I'm afraid of being caught, but because my own voice seems to have been sucked from me.

Holy. Hell.

Feeling the end is near, I whimper, "Drew..."

His tongue pushes at my entrance before the tip teases my clit into submission. In a harsh breath my body trembles on top of his tongue, feeding the brute appetite he seems to have. Without allowing me a moment to catch my breath, Drew's dick invades my still pulsating pussy, in sheer declaration. Arching upward, I grip the sides of the table for leverage as he roughly thrusts repeatedly. Lost in the furor of the sex, my eyes shut and surrender to the pleasure being passed between us. Suddenly my pussy starts to tighten. Drew's cock swells in response. Before either of us can stop, our orgasms erupt causing savage cries and callings to echo in the greenhouse.

Completely spent, I fall forward again, thankful the table is there to catch me. After my breath starts to settle, Drew slowly pulls out. "Is that how you really apologize?"

He lightly chuckles. "I don't know. I've never really had to say it often to anyone other than my brothers."

Just as my lips turn upward, there's a cloth cleaning the remains of our latest tryst. "You're really good at that."

"At what, baby?"

"All of that." I giggle. Feeling my pants being pushed at my feet, I step into them as I'm directed. "Like really good." Once they're securely up, I turn around and question, "How'd you get so good?"

Drew who's already tucked his dick away replies, "Lots of practice."

A brief concern that should've hit me sooner comes to mind. "Should-"

"Clean," he cuts me off. "I had a shot of EA the morning I was kidnapped."

I was here that morning. Mixing the very thing that's going to tear us apart.

"What about...birth control?" Drew barely breathes out. "Ya know, little mini McCoys someday might not be a bad thing, but right now-"

"I'm sterile," I blurt out.

The sadness that fills his brown eyes is one I battled in my own for months.

Any longer and suicide would've been more than just a constant passing thought. Maybe I should've just done it. At least it wouldn't be me killing him, right? I'm gonna stop that. I promise. I just...I have to tell him first and after that, he might actually trust me enough to let me fix the mess I've made.

"What?"

"There's a sterilizing shot that I was given when I first got here." My fingers toy with the end of my braid. "They told me it was for the flu, but I wasn't that stupid. Eventually The Devil explained how it was best in case I ever decided to give in and explore the options around me. He couldn't afford to have me pregnant."

Rage replaces the sadness as he nods. "One more reason to kill him."

Did we need another?

"So if we want kids some day-"

Swiftly my hand lands gently on his cheek. "One step at a time. Let's focus on getting out of this alive before we start discussing the idea of procreation."

He smiles against my hand. "Alright."

With one more hum and a quick peck, I move past him back the direction we traveled from. I check the contents of the case one final time before shutting it. Once it's closed, I nod my head the direction of the cottage.

As we enter the house, we're startled to see Rex inside, arms folded tightly across his chest. With an irritated look he snaps, "Where the fuck were you two?"

"In Eden," I bite back. "Unlike you I require a little more subtlety for my weapons of pain."

"I like to think you require a little more subtlety for more than that," Rex tries to flirt, which causes Drew to tense beside me.

"You wouldn't know," Drew snaps.

Rex growls, "You wouldn't fucking know either." His eyes lower to a glare, "And you? Why the fuck were you out there?"

"Dinner," he states without missing a beat. "Needed to know if she was cooking before she left or if I needed to fend for myself."

"What are *you* doing here?" I redirect the conversation. "Omar's picking me up."

"Yeah. He said he was on his way. I'm here to babysit," he sneers at me. "So since she's not cooking you can eat shit for dinner."

"Maybe you eat what you are, but I'm more a pizza man myself," Drew's joke gets a smile from me.

Nonchalantly I point. "There's a frozen pizza in there for you."

He nods slowly his eyes getting swept away in mine. Rex clears his throat.

Shit. We have to stop acting like that where actual people can see.

Turning back to him I snip, "Maybe if you're nice, he'll share with you."

Drew whispers behind his hand, "Probably not."

I chuckle and roll my eyes. "Whatever. I have to shower. I'll see you tomorrow, Drew."

Rex grunts, poorly hiding his jealousy. "Drew?"

"Believe it or not McCoy is my *last* name." The smart ass remark is proceeded with him shooting me one final smile. "See ya then."

Walking away with the briefcase dangling from my grip, I try to hide the glow I'm sure is painted on my face. In my doorway, I give Drew one final glance to see him give me a small eyebrow rise.

Yup. Definitely have to shower away this momentary joy. The Devil senses happiness even faster than he senses fear. Do me a favor and remind me of that tonight when my brain wanders to its happy place in desperation to forget the person I'm helping him kill at dinner.

Drew

Waking up with Melody just in the house is better than most things I've experienced in my life. As pussy whipped as that sounds it's fucking true. Just knowing I can roll out of bed and see her face within minutes of being awake is amazing, which makes it equally as fucking hard when she's not here.

I head across the living room for the kitchen passing a snoring Rex. Unhappy to see he's still here, I grunt.

Honestly, I'm not surprised. I waited up as long as I could last night for Melody to get home. What? Can you blame me? Fuck, I would've snuck into her room and recreated that magic moment she did for me.

Seeing the two tablets and glass of water for me on the counter causes my heart to sink.

She was here and left already. Fuck.

"Take your pills prisoner," Rex says on a yawn.

Add him to the list of people I wanna shoot. What! He shot me first!

After swallowing them, thankful she knew I would probably still be sore, I turn around. "Is Melody the only person that's pleasant?"

"Don't get attached to her," he bites. "You're lifespan is much shorter than you wanna believe it is."

I bite my tongue.

"You can't possibly be dumb enough to think you're gonna make it out of this job alive." When I don't answer he laughs, shakes his head, and closes his eyes. "Pathetic. Almost as pathetic as thinking you'll get to runaway into the sunset with the princess. Grow the fuck up. Even if you had a shot of making it out of this alive, she'd rather kill herself than end up with pathetic street trash like you McCoy."

Resisting the urge to throw the glass at him, I place it on the counter, and grab an apple to crunch on.

Oh his time is coming. Stay cool. We'll handle that motherfucker together.

The morning seems to fly by quicker than I predicted. I spend most of it working on the custom features for the person we are supposed to be impersonating.

This dude has some of the thickest fucking eyebrows I've ever seen in my life. It's ridiculous. All together the dude is really fucking hairy. I mean, I wanna buy him a goddamn razor myself.

My brush carefully fills in another line next to the actual hair as the front door opens. I glance up to see my girl walking in, the sight of her in jeans and a white t-shirt almost as fucking sexy as her in those scrubs.

I say almost because now I know she doesn't wear fucking panties under that shit. What? No. Eyes up. Don't worry about my hard on.

She folds her arms at the sight of Rex. "Comfy?"

His feet fall off the table. "Babysitting is boring."

"Well good thing you have a delivery to make," Melody announces.

Her eyes don't move my direction. The action makes my body tense. Wanting her attention, but knowing it's not something I should flip out about, I drop my eyes back to painting.

The sound of them shuffling around causes me to glance up again to see them disappear into her room.

I really fucking hate that he's in there. I haven't even been in there.

Uncomfortable with the idea of him alone with her, the idea of rape gnawing at the back of my throat, causes me to shift in my seat in a sad attempt to see inside. Thankfully she strolls out in a hurry straight for the fridge. Casually I let my eyes fall before they notice me watching them.

"To Nina." Her announcement grabs my attention unconsciously.

Nina is the chick that's babysitting Daniel. Is it wrong I hope he's getting to experience at least a little of what I am right now?

"Straight there, Rex. She needs to give that to him today. Immediately. Do you understand?"

"Why do you talk to me like I'm slow?" Rex whines.

She folds her arms across her chest. "Your shoes are untied."

He looks down. "Really?"

"They're velcro," she sighs.

I chuckle under my breath.

Point proven. He's an idiot.

"Go," she rushes him out. "Bag to Nina. Brief case to JJ. Nina first."

"I heard you," he snaps and then looks over at me. "Why aren't you fucking working?"

"Why aren't you?" I poke back.

Rex makes a move for me and Mel sharply snaps her fingers. She points like she's talking to a dog that's misbehaving. "Now."

He mutters something and stalks out of the cottage. After he slams the door shut I say, "You should get him neutered." When she snickers a little my world seems to align just right again. "I've missed that sound."

Melody leans her back against the closed fridge door. "Oh yeah?"

"Fuck yeah," I confirm, placing the paint brush down, but not moving.

"Miss anything else?"

"Other than the sight of you prancing around this place in scrubs-"

"I don't prance," she interrupts on another giggle.

"You prance."

"I do not."

With a wide smile I state, "It would be easier to ask me what I didn't miss about you being here."

"Which is?"

"Nothing."

A small swoon comes out of her. "I've missed you too."

"Good." Pushing the piece away from me to dry, I ask, "What time did you get in?"

"This morning," she answers. "It all ran fairly late and Omar figured I could crash at his apartment. I got in early this morning with a long list of things to fix and deliver, so I didn't get to make you breakfast."

"You can make it up to me later," I assure. "Dinner?"

Mel nods. "Definitely dinner."

Relieved she will be around for that I ask, "Speaking of...how was last night?"

Doing her best to pretend whatever she witnessed didn't frighten her as much as it did, she clears her throat. "Turns out The Devil had the prince you're impersonating kidnapped last night. I um...delivered the Mind Erasers for it."

"Mind Erasers?"

"It's basically a combination of drugs that erases your short term memory. It's mixed with a hallucinogen, so that you're not certain if what you've experienced is real or not, *if* you even remember at all." My jaw drops but I'm not sure how to respond. "Typically it's what I give if we kidnap someone and plan to set them free. The Devil doesn't kill as often as you would think. Hell until recently it was only when necessary."

"And now?"

"I think it's a combination of spite, frustration, and fear."

"The Devil afraid?" I chortle. "Of what?"

"Losing everything. His empire is falling and he can't find the brick causing it to collapse." She briefly looks away. "Last night...last night he poisoned another cop insisting desperate times call for desperate measures."

Preaching to the choir on that one.

"He knows it's not you McCoys, which just pisses him off more."

"How does he know that?"

"Video footage," she sighs.

There's a long quiet pause before I cautiously ask, "Nina is the one taking care of my brother, right?"

Melody tries to hide her nervousness. "Yes."

"Is he okay?"

Her eyes flash the temptation to lie.

"Tell me the truth."

"He....he could be doing better." Quickly she adds, "He will. As soon as she gets that package." Before I can ask any more questions, she heads towards the back door. "I have to take care of a few things, but I'll see you for dinner, alright?"

I wiggle my eyebrows. "And dessert."

Melody rolls her eyes before disappearing. Once she's gone panic tries to settle in my chest.

What do you think is wrong with Daniel? Do you know? Do you think he's suffering from weird aches and pains like me? I swear it's just the mattresses or maybe the stress of all this, but that look in her eyes reminds me of the one I see when Omar is around. The dark side of the moon. Just...just do me a favor and if you know something let me in on it? We're family. That's what we do.

**

My forehead hits the glass door with a frown. The rain continues to pour violently, beating up the patio and erasing the corner of privacy we've found.

Fucking. Rain.

"No matter how hard you pout, it's not going anywhere," Melody announces from behind me. "Now come eat."

On a sigh, I turn to see her placing two plates down on the coffee table. "I really wanted to have dinner where prying eyes couldn't catch us."

"Shit happens." She shrugs nonchalantly. "Just be grateful we get to eat together at all tonight."

"True." I sit down across from her on the floor. Glancing over the BBQ chicken and mashed potatoes makes me smile.

Reminds me a little of home. We're almost out of here. Just hold on a little longer. And a little tighter.

My fork damn near jumps in my hand. "Looks better than frozen pizza."

She snickers. "You act like you've never eaten frozen pizza before?"

"I've eaten more of that shit than could possibly be healthy for a person." When she giggles again I declare, "However nothing compares to having a home cooked meal by the hottest chick you've ever seen in your life."

Instead of rolling her eyes like I expect, she bites her bottom lip. A groan comes from me. I adjust my crotch.

Could you stop looking down there? It's not polite to stare.

Dinner conversation progresses the way it normally does. She asks questions about life out from under The Devil's thumb and I tell tales of the crazy stunts me and my brothers have completed on and off our bikes. Memories from all the McCoys, dead and alive, flow from my mouth to her ears at such a rate, she stops eating to get lost in the stories. For once instead of feeling like just another part of the McCoy clan, I feel like the most important member. I feel like I'm king of the world and top shit.

Strange considering I'm being held hostage, but let's just let that go.

"Knox sounds amazing," Melody giggles and pushes her plate away. "Except..."

"Except what?"

"Except, well, okay. Why is she just waiting around for Madden like that?"

"Tricky question. You'd have to ask her."

"Well, why does he treat her like that?"

"Trickier answer," I mumble and lean back on my palms. "I don't think he wants too. I think what happens more often than people care to admit, is you wear a mask. You put on the face people expect to see. You start living up to the expectations of your name or reputation or expected behavior and the real you stays hidden. I think sometimes you wanna take it off. Show the world who you really are, but are afraid they won't like it. That they'll reject you or even worse, you'll reject you. You'll start to hate the person behind the mask because you've worn it so long that's the real you and the person you thought you were hiding either no longer exists or would just be a different mask for you to wear because you have no idea who you really are any more." Looking down at my empty plate on the coffee table I whisper, "Or maybe that's just me..."

"It's not just you," she confirms. "Being Triple D is your mask, isn't it?"

Her question lifts my eyes back up.

"Do you know who Drew is?"

"After almost ten days of being just him? I think so."

She curls her lips into a smile. "If it matters, you'll always be Drew to me. That's who I'll always see."

See what I mean? How could I walk away from her? How could I want her anywhere else but with me?

The lights shut off as thunder rocks the house. While the outage is very brief, it's enough to get my mind wandering. "Back up?"

"Eden has back up generators."

"But the cameras?"

She smiles again as she shakes her head.

Come on Thor! Knock that power out again so I can knock that pussy out in peace. What? Of course I really just said that.

Melody stands. "I'm going to do the dishes and read on the couch for a bit."

I rise and attempt to grab dishes. "Will I see you later?"

With a flick of her wrist, she shoos me away. "Yes. Now go. Just in case we have an audience, we should keep up the usual routine."

After a short nod, I start to walk backwards towards my room. "Night Mel..."

While heading towards the sink, she calls back without turning around, "Night Drew."

Knowing there's a thunderstorm prevents me from my normal routine of scrubbing away the art leftovers of the day. Instead, I give my teeth a good brush, shed my clothes and crawl into bed. The anticipation of her in my bed is enough to feed my mind for hours, but the minor aches that seem to occur before I crash are already beginning. For a few I lie still willing them away. At first thoughts about the different places I can't wait to fuck her outside this place flood my brain. Before my dick can't handle being any harder, I switch to the idea of showing her around the McCoy mechanic shop. Introducing her to my brothers. Explaining to her Madden and Knoxie both bark a lot harder than they bite...well, to friends of the family anyway. I start to consider what she might find to talk to Destin about. Easily my mind starts to float towards Daniel, the idea that he's fucked up without help clawing at more than my conscious.

I can't lose another brother. I won't.

Eventually I drift off to sleep figuring it's a better idea to rest a little since I won't be the rest of the night. I'm not sure how long I'm out before Melody enters the room, but the minute the bed dips beside me, I swiftly roll on top of her.

She giggles, "You were dead asleep."

"Parts of me," I yawn as my cock that sensed her before I did nudges between her legs. The second it brushes against her dripping wet panty-less pussy a groan creeps out of me. "Damn, Mel. I missed you."

"Missed me or *parts* of me," her playful counter is followed with her wrapping her arms around my neck.

On a grunt, I remove her hands and pin them above her head. My knees part her legs and without further warning I thrust harshly inside. Her body arches off the bed. With my lips beside her ear I declare. "You."

"Drew," she whimpers as I pump once more, her pussy determined to swallow more and more of me with each push provided.

Releasing her hands, I place my lips greedily over hers and start making up for lost time with my tongue. Our mouths fuse together determined to match the speed of our frenzied hips. Between ardent kisses, my hands roam her soft skin, her nipples easily requiring more attention than anything else.

Come on...we haven't spent that much time together.

When I tug softly, her mouth slips from mine and she cries my name loudly.

It's like body bingo.

My pumping slows down as I draw my body slightly upward anxious to hear her make those sounds again. I roll my fingers across her other nipple and repeat the action. She bucks her hips and mewls for more. The small but effective torture has me smiling and wishing I could see this in more light.

When we get out of this place, we are never fucking in the dark again.

Once I've had my fill of her begging, I drape her legs over my shoulders. She tenses at the new position. "Relax baby. I'll take care of you."

"It's so deep, Drew," she whimpers, her muscles trying to expel my dick, the tight pulses making it hard not to fuck the shit out of her like this. "I don't think I can take it..."

"I." My lips kiss her calf. "Promise." I kiss the other one. "You. Can." With a gentle scraping of my teeth against her ankle, her pussy welcomes my cock. Slowly I plunge deeper, my eyes shutting in pure rhapsody. The pumping continues in long drawn-out motions, wanting her to feel everything I can offer as much as wanting to experience everything she's awarding me.

And trust me. Her pussy is a prized piece. Not just because it's so tight, but because it's a perfect fit for me. Do you know how rare that shit is?

When I slip my thumb to her clit to assist in making her come, she moans her hands gripping my biceps. "Make me come, Drew...."

With a crooked smirk I whisper, "Always baby."

I rub in the pressured circles I know she enjoys while I continue to push deeply. It doesn't take long before her body is a withering mess. The sound of her breath being lost acts as the best aphrodisiac a guy could dream of.

Not that I needed any help.

"I'm coming," she cries out loudly, her moans easily now screams, the shaking of the house in tandem with her body. "Drew!"

Overwhelmed by it all, I drop her legs, so she can wrap them around my waist. In her ear I command, "Again. Call my name out again."

"Drew!" Her lips effortlessly sing the hymn with each jackhammer of my hips.

The repetition cultivates the ravenous beast she's created inside. I thrust harder and harder, shamelessly saying, "I'm gonna mark your body, Mel. It's mine." Her flexing muscles that are warning another orgasm is near cause me to growl. "It belongs to me. *You* belong to me, Mel." The throbbing of her pussy starts milking my weeping dick. "And *I* belong to you..." At that moment a hot surge fills her as cries of devotion leave us both reverberating with such force I'm not sure who is making more sound, the storm or us.

In one swift motion, I drop onto my back, pulling her frame over to embrace mine. With my arms tucked tightly around her, I plant a kiss on her forehead. The feeling of her face smiling against my chest has me feeling like I'm in paradise.

"Does the house have power?"

"No," she sighs, her fingertips stroking my abs.

Desperate and not afraid to show it, I beg, "Will you stay the night with me then? Here. In my bed."

I can feel the apprehension that often arises, return. "Drew-"

"Please, Melody." Feeling my own explainable fear, I plead, "I need you tonight...."

The room falls silent to voices, the beating rain seeming more like it's punching the house rather than falling on it.

"Is this about Daniel?" Hearing his name stops my hands from stroking her shoulder. "Are you worried about him?"

"Yeah," I quietly confess. "And losing you. Every time you leave, I worry The Devil's gonna do something and I might not see you again. Maybe that makes me a pussy-"

"It doesn't."

"Well I feel like a pussy," I mutter under my breath. "Could you just...sleep with me for a bit? You can sneak out before the sun rises, but can I have that part of you just once?"

Her chin pops up on my chest. However she doesn't say anything.

Talk about deafening silence.

"I'll stay, but we have to talk in the morning, okay?"

Worry tries to battle with the sleep that wants to settle in. "About what? Is something wrong? Should I-"

"Just rest, Drew."

"But-"

"Rest Drew...just trust me and rest."

"Okay," I whisper on another yawn shutting my eyes. "Thank you for you staying, Mel."

And thanks to you too. You've been a good friend this entire time. Thanks for keeping it real with me. Oh, and thanks for keeping me company in the world's weirdest prison cell.

Melody

A word to the wise. Bliss in The Devil's world is always a short lived state.

"Don't you two look comfortable," his voice springs my body upward.

Oh. Shit. Oh shit.

He compliments with a cigar dangling from his lips, "Beautiful rack might I add." I reach for the sheet to wrap around me just as Drew starts to stir. "Much better than the one I saw last night."

"Eyes off my girl," Drew's growl isn't as impressive through the large yawn he's exhibiting.

"Your girl?" The Devil chuckles. "That's cute. Isn't that cute, Omar?"

My head whips around to see Omar with a displeased expression leaning against the door frame. "Disgusting."

"Such a sour kitten that one," The Devil says while shaking his head. "Honestly, I think it's cute McCoy. You've fallen for the girl *actively* killing you."

Shame forces my head down.

Drew questions, "Huh?"

"I know you McCoys are a little slow, but you can't possibly be *that* slow." When Drew doesn't say anything else, The Devil sighs, "You bunch give me a headache. It's why you'll never sit at the top of the mountain."

"What. Do. You. Mean. Killing. Me?"

"Your skin discoloration. The aches. The pains. All results of the poison you've been ingesting every morning thanks to Eve."

My eyes fall closed.

No. He's not lying. Yes. You can hate me now. But I was going to heal him! Let me explain-

"P-p-poison?" Drew barely spews.

"Yes. That little vixen in your bed has been killing you and your brother since you two arrived. Isn't that right?" I don't reply, which makes him repeat, "Isn't that right, Eve?"

"Yes," I whisper.

"No. No. Look at me," The Devil commands my face upward. "I like to look at my weapons in all their glory."

With tears falling from my eyes as much as they are down the back of my throat I stare at the man who has made me into the killer I am.

"Is your name really Eve? Not Melody?" Drew snaps at me. I turn my head and he bites, "You've been fucking lying to me this whole time haven't you?"

"I-"

"Here's what's interesting," The Devil grabs our attention again. Leaning back in his seat he scrunches his face. "Either little Eve hasn't been giving you the proper dose or your brother's immune system is weaker than yours. Check out what Eve's creation has done to him...or should be doing to you."

The screen splits to Daniel who is laying in bed an almost green color, sweating profusely, shaking uncontrollably while Nina dabs his forehead with a towel.

In a barely audible tone, Drew croaks, "Daniel..."

"Beautiful isn't it?" The Devil chortles as the other shot vanishes. "She really is a whiz at this shit." He ashes his cigar. "If it makes you feel any better, you're not the only guy she's ever slept with *and* killed. You know...I don't miss Jimmy."

I can explain that too. I can! I-

"Now if you keep up your end of the deal McCoy, there will be a beautiful antidote waiting for you, courtesy of the same woman beside you." The Devil smirks. "I'm not even mad at you for fucking a McCoy Eve. I'm almost impressed you've finally started to reap some of the benefits of your job position." Before I can say anything else he states, "Thank you, Omar. You know what to do next."

"Yes sir," Omar replies.

"See you two very soon..."

The second the screen is shut off, I turn to Drew, voice pleading, "I can-"

"Get out." He coldly states, head hung.

"Drew-"

"Out!" His scream causes more tears to come from me. "Now!"

Yanking the sheet to keep my body covered, I hold it closed and rush from the room.

I deserve that and so much more. I just...I need to explain. I can explain. Will you listen? Um...hello?

"Melody." Omar's voice states as I cross the living room for my own bedroom. "Melody."

I don't respond. Once I'm in my room, I head straight for the bathroom to clean up since I'm most likely about to be dragged from here to my demise.

Fine. Don't listen to me about anything else, but hear me now. The Devil is not okay with me sleeping with Drew. He's livid.

How I'm going to die just went from quick and meaningless to slow with lots of torture. And since you are somewhat listening, I tried to tell you I was going to heal Drew! I wasn't going to just let him die like The Devil has planned.

"Melody. Stop." Omar's demand turns my body around, hand still on the door knob.

"What?"

In a low, almost hurt tone, he shakes his head. "How could you fucking do that?"

I press my lips together.

"How could you not fucking listen to me? How could you throw your life away for a McCoy? For a fucking McCoy."

"He is so much more than the disgusting tag line that is his name."

"If you believe that then you're even more naive than I thought."

"Or maybe," I snip and lift my eyebrows. "Maybe I'm not fucking stupid enough to believe everything I'm told. Maybe I did a little research myself-"

"You let him research between your legs."

"Fuck. You." My curse stumbles him backwards. "Don't you dare stand there and judge me."

"How can I not?" Omar whispers. "You gave up your life for a quick fuck. You're a dead woman now."

"I've been a dead woman for a very long time." The tears that had paused begin again. "Just because your heart is beating doesn't mean you're alive."

"Melody-"

"I've been dead for years, just waiting for my moment. For my time card to be punched." Taking a step forward I state, "You know what I did? I took the power away from The Devil. *I* picked when my life is over and if I was given the chance to do my time with Drew over the only thing I would change is I would've started sleeping with him sooner."

Omar's surprised expression actually feels good.

Well as good as it can knowing the person you actually love in the world now hates you.

"Now, I need to shower. Chances are if you are here that means it's to drag me somewhere. I would like to be clean first."

Omar clears his throat. "I'm not."

"What?"

"I'm not here to take you anywhere." Seeing the look of confusion on my face he sighs, "The Devil figured because of the power outages last night, the cameras might've needed to be reset. He knows how much you hate fucking with them so he sent me out."

Basically my own distaste for that chore got me caught. Wow. My fucking luck.

Trying to hide my own hurt, I ask, "Why did you rat me out?"

"It wasn't intentional." He confesses. "I was fucking with the power and when the cameras came back on, The Devil immediately spotted you." Omar sighs, "I can't save you."

Instead of being understanding, I ask, "If you could, would you?" His eyes flicker and what I had been afraid of hit me like a ton of bricks. "I didn't think so..."

The only thing sadder than being completely alone in the world, is the moment you realize it.

Melody

At least you're listening to me now. I tried to talk to Drew yesterday and nothing. I wasn't surprised, not even a little, but spent most of the day crying as a result. You know what's even worse? He wouldn't come out to eat or drink anything. He needs to. Even if I have to force feed it to him. If he doesn't he's going to be dying a lot faster without giving me a chance to save him. Like I told you and have been trying to tell you, I'm not gonna keep killing him. I wanna heal him.

With a heavy knock, I forcefully say, "Open the door, Drew."

There's no response.

I could just open the door because there aren't locks on them, but I'm not trying to make the situation worse.

"Open the door, Drew. Now."

To my surprise this time he yanks it open. His usually strong frame looks like it's seconds from tumbling over. His skin looks washed out. There's a distinct blood shot hue to his eyes from constant vomiting.

My hand twitches to touch him. I wait for him to say something. Anything. Finally I offer him the glass I'm holding and the pills. "Take. These."

His eyes glare. "Get that shit the fuck out of my face."

Holding my ground and more importantly my tears at bay I shove them at him. "Stop being so fucking stubborn and take them." He doesn't move. "You look like shit. Feel like hell. Take them, so you can feel better."

Cruelly he says, "As in when I'm a dead man?"

In a weak whisper I demand, "Take. Them."

Drew gives the pills one final look before reaching for them. He gulps them down with the glass of water and shoves it back at me. "You can go now."

"No." I firmly state. Surprised his eyebrows dart down. "I gave you all the space you needed yesterday. Today, you eat. You drink. You live to escape the fuck out of this place. Now get dressed or don't but breakfast is on the table."

He rubs the back of his neck clearly on the cusp of passing out. With a shrug he says, "I guess I should eat something."

Swiftly he moves past me and heads for the kitchen table where pancakes, eggs, and bacon are waiting for him.

What can I say? Just trying to make it all easier...

As soon as he sits down at the table he sneers, "Peace offering? Pathetic."

"I deserve that," I reply sitting beside him. Picking up my coffee cup I sigh, "I deserve a lot. So hit me with it. Yell at me. Scream at me. Tell me what a shitty person I am, but at the end, I need you to listen to what I have to say."

Hesitantly he reaches for his fork. "Talk."

Surprised he's not ripping me apart, I choke out, "Huh?"

"You wanna explain or justify killing me and my brother. Go ahead. Talk."

"Aren't you gonna-"

"Walk out of this room if you don't start explaining and start explaining fast? Yeah." Before I have a chance to say anything he snaps, "Tell me he was lying. Tell me you haven't been killing me since I walked through the door."

My fingers clink the side of the mug. "Not exactly."

The pointed look pushes me to continue.

"You're given two tablets every morning. One is the poison, the other is like an antidote. Not enough to cure you but enough to slow down and mask the symptoms you should be experiencing."

"So Daniel's dying faster because you're not fucking him?"

Hearing the harsh nature of his sentence I put my cup down. "No. He's dying faster because he's either not taking them like he should or he's only taking one instead of both. The purpose was to kill you slowly and after it was all finished the 'antidote' is the final dose to end your life. It wouldn't be enough for you to just fall out, so much as die in front of your brother's eyes."

His jaw slips open.

It's okay. You can be speechless too.

"I've been working on an actual antidote for you and your brother. One you can take home and immediately use to cancel out what The Devil wants you to take." Drew's mouth twitches. "I've also swapped the poison pill for two antidotes. I was going to sooner, but I wasn't here that morning then your brother got extra sick and I just hadn't had the chance."

"The Devil is going to notice."

"Use some of your paints and to create a similar discoloring and continue to fake the symptoms. No one will know the difference."

Drew leans back in his seat, food still untouched.

"You need to eat. You're body will heal faster."

"Why did you do it to begin with?" He questions.

"It was my job," I answer. "This is what he keeps me for. Well kept me for. I'm a dead woman now."

Confused he tilts his head in question.

"You know in this lifestyle there are only two choices. Kill. Or be killed." With a shrug and tears in my eyes I sigh, "I'm tired of helping kill people. I'm tired of living under The Devil's reign. And after just days with you, I knew I would rather die than be responsible for killing you or your brother."

"But-"

"The sacrifice you make for love, I guess." My eyes glance down at my cup in an attempt to gain my composure. "Fact is, everything is a choice. Even when there are nothing but bad choices, with no possible way out, you still have to choose. A choice still has to be made." I sniffle. "You deserve to live more than I do."

So do you.

Suddenly there's a hand on my thigh. I drag my eyes upward.

"You don't deserve to die either."

I try to offer him a smile. "I can't say I agree."

"Mel-"

"I'm sorry," my voice chokes out. "For everything. For not telling you sooner. For having to hurt you and your brother in the first place."

"Thank you for saving us."

"Haven't saved you yet..."

"But you will." Drew squeezes my thigh with one hand and finally lifts his fork with the other. "And that's what matters." When the corner of my lip turns upward he says, "Promise you won't try to kill me again."

"No promises if you cheat on me..."

He chuckles reminding of me just how much I've missed that sound.

I love this side of him even more than I love the naked side. I know. Hard to believe. You've seen him naked. He's like a modern tattooed Adonis.

"I swear to never cheat on you. You're the only woman I wanna spend the rest of my life with."

Hearing the words out loud causes new tears.

He will spend the rest of my short lived life with me. Bittersweet isn't it?

"And you're gonna make it out of this alive with me. Got it?" I nod and he has a bite of eggs moaning as they hit his pallet. After a few more bites he says, "Tell me about Jimmy."

The sound of his name causes my body to go rigid. Drew immediately gives my leg a comforting rub.

"Honesty. That's the only way we can move forward."

You agree?

A deep exhale escapes me. "I met Jimmy while I was working on my Master's Degree. On one of the few nights I was invited for a drink with my classmates, I went. He was there. He reminded me of a younger Benicio Del Toro. Women flocked to him, but he flocked to me." Shaking my head slowly, I glare at the memory. "Thinking back on it now, it's obvious he was playing me from the beginning. Anyway, he wined me and dined me. Typical shy girl falling for the first guy to pay attention to her. Eventually he told me, he had a friend who needed a favor."

"The Devil."

"Sneaky as shit even then. We met and he offered me a job. Said he needed someone with my specific skill set. Turns out Jimmy was his 'Find It' man. He went out and found whoever it was The Devil needed. This time, a medicine maker. I had two choices. I could accept the job and the riches and live or deny him and be killed. On the spot."

"Sounds about right."

"So desperate to live, I agreed to do whatever it was he needed me too. At first, it was just little jobs. Pain killers. Healing aids. Then he had me start creating things to shut down memories. Then organs. Eventually, he saw the opportunity of a lifetime, which is when he kidnapped me from my apartment in the middle of the night and stuck me here. Made the whole thing look like I ran away and eloped with Jimmy. Only my mother didn't believe it. By that time Eden was slowly under way, but I created the rest. He told me I could have whatever I wanted." In a whisper I snap, "Anything but my life back."

"What happened to Jimmy?"

"Like a hopeless idiot I tried to give him more chances in the beginning. I didn't want to believe he was that horrible. I wanted to believe there was still good in him. Eventually though, no matter how hard I tried to hide from it, I couldn't any more. Jimmy's biggest flaw besides lying was being greedy. He always wanted more. One day The Devil found out Jimmy was stealing from him. He had me create something he named 'Hail Mary'. It's a nasty poison. The first time I created it, he invited me to see the effects in person. He also failed to mention the person it would be used on was Jimmy. I watched as he injected it into him. I was forced to watch him die before my eyes. At the very end of it all, The Devil made sure to let me know I needed to be careful with the choices I made in his world or I could end up like Jimmy."

Drew ceased eating. Slowly he takes my hand and lifts it to lips. "I'm not gonna let you end up like Jimmy. I promise."

I offer him the reassuring smile he needs.

As much as I want to believe him, I know better. It's not that I don't trust him. It's that I know what The Devil is capable of. He's always three steps ahead. Chances are he's already got everything set up in place for my death, so I'm gonna do the only thing I can. Save the man I love and enjoy my dying days.

Drew

What do you do when it feels like there's no right answer? What do you do when you're not sure you can trust the person you love most in the world? Yeah. Yeah. I know. I have no business saying that bullshit. Spending a week with someone, chances are it's not love is what you're thinking. Well fuck you for that. You're willing to give up your own life to let them live? That's love. I believe everything Mel told me a couple days ago. Hell, she even made good on her word of slipping me antidote she hid in various places to make it less obvious in case we are being watched. The aspirin bottle. Back of the fridge behind fruit I could hide it with. Underneath my napkin. I don't think for one minute she ever wanted to kill me or Daniel for that matter. I don't even blame her for not telling me sooner. I hate that she didn't. I hate that she didn't trust that I would save her, that I'm going to get her out of this hell hole. And I'm gonna get us out. I just hope when we're on the other side, when we have a chance to start over, she actually starts to trust me. I hope I can start to trust her. Can you be in love with someone you don't trust? That doesn't trust you? How about this? Can you rebuild trust with someone you love?

"You're thinking too hard," Melody calls to me.

I look up to see her leaned against the kitchen counter.

"I can tell by the way your forehead wrinkles."

My eyes roll.

It's doesn't wrinkle. No. No it doesn't.

"Wanna talk about it?"

On a heavy sigh I push the finished sculpture I'll be delivering tomorrow away from me. "Not really."

She nods. Silence settles between us once more.

There have been lots of these moments since she confessed everything. Every time I get to a point of understanding, Daniel's face pops back in my head and anger takes it's place. Mistrust invades. Doubt that this is some sick move by the man who always seems to be ahead of everything.

"Just say it," she whispers. "Just admit it, Drew."

"Admit what?"

"You think you love me, but still don't trust me."

I pause. "Do you blame me?"

Melody folds her arms. "No." When I look away she adds, "And I don't blame you if you've changed your mind."

Confused, I lift my eyebrows. "About what?"

"About trying to save me."

"Mel-"

"I deserve to die for what I've done. And honestly? I would rather die than spend the rest of my life having to wake up to the look that's in your eyes right now." Shocked at the words, my jaw cracks open. "I don't blame you for feeling the way you are. I don't blame you if you feel this way for a while, but I can't go on forever with you never truly forgiving me. So tell me that now, Drew. Can you really forgive me some day?"

Our eyes lock. The air in the room feels like it's being sucked out. Breathing doesn't even seem like it's more necessary than answering that question. Nothing is more important than answering that question.

Can I? Can I forgive her? Fuck. Can I blame her? If the situation was reversed, what would I have done? What about you? Aren't our brains wired to survive first and consider the consequences or hurt feelings second? We've all done shit we're not proud of to survive. Hurt others in the process. When life forces you to make the only moves you have, you do what's necessary. That's understandable. That's forgivable.

I extend my hand out for her to take. "Come here."

With a hard swallow, she swipes away the tears on her cheeks and strolls over to me.

As soon as she arrives, I pull her into my lap, legs straddled around me. I touch the end of her braid. "Do you trust me?"

There's no hesitation. "Yes."

Nodding I instruct, "Undo your braid." She gives me a skeptical look, but follows my directions. When her hair is free from the braid, I run my finger through it for the first time. She shutters from the touch, eyes closing. In a whisper I question, "Do you care that The Devil's watching?"

"No," she sighs as my fingers comb through it softly. "The only thing I care about is you."

Pleased by her answer I pull her forehead down to mine by the nape of her neck. My voice falls to a hushed tone. "I hate what you did to me and my brother."

Tears begins to land in our laps. "I'm so sorry..."

"I know, baby," I sniffle my own pending tears away. "I know you only did what you had too. I can't hate you for trying to survive. Please...please don't ever give me another reason not to trust you."

More tears drop. "I won't. I swear."

"Good." Tilting my lips up to hers I finish with, "Because I don't wanna regret falling in love with you, Mel."

Our mouths softly join for just a moment. To my surprise she pulls away and whispers back, "I love you too, Drew."

Fueled by relief as much as remorse, our actions become passionately hectic. Clothes begin to fly off. Our teeth bump together during kisses so brutal they could bruise. In the fanatical whirlwind in which we are so desperate to stop being separate entities, all other emotions outside of love disperse. The second my cock pushes inside Mel and she screams in pleasure, I know the only thing that matters is making it out alive together. Living the rest of our lives on the same team. Every pump is delivered with so much warmth I can feel her body being washed clean of The Devil. Her arms clamp around my neck. My teeth bite and mark her perfect skin. She sways her hips back and forth, seducing my orgasm to expose itself before hers. Finding this unacceptable, I abruptly stop, lift her up and lay her down, her back pressed against the table. I spread her thighs wide, gripping them tightly as I ram repeatedly into her.

During the roughness I roar, "Fuck!"

"Yes!" she shouts back, the simple action proving to me where her loyalty lies. Her pussy all of sudden clamps down on my cock, exploding with damn near no warning. Quiver after quiver seeps out of her, drowning my cock in a vortex of euphoria.

In several long waves come floods her tight pussy. I rumble, "Mel..."

Melody's body seems to accept the offering with welcoming squeezes. There's desperation in the gripping, almost as much as in her hands, which are clawing at my body to cover hers. When I fall forward, she arches upward, lips landing next to my ear, "I love you, Drew McCoy."

Through my panting, I question, "Promise?"

"Promise."

Drew

I adjust the collar to my suit jacket.

Why do people wear these willingly?

"It fine," Melody hums from my bedroom door way. "Really."

"Why do I feel like I have a rash on my neck?"

She rolls her eyes. "Maybe because you usually don't wear shirts so it's a huge adjustment to wear not only a shirt, but a jacket. Not one collar, but two...."

Her playful sarcasm causes me to shoot her an equally playful nasty glare. "Ha-Ha."

With a glance over her shoulder she asks, "Do you have it?"

"Yeah."

"The Devil is going to be tracking you every step of the way," she starts slowly. "There's a GPS tracking device planted in your leg."

In disbelief I snap, "You didn't think to tell me sooner?"

"If I had, would you have tried to remove it?"

Who wouldn't?

"Exactly. That would've tipped The Devil off faster that something was wrong. It was about keeping up appearances remember?"

Flopping on the edge of my bed I ask, "How hard is it to remove?"

"You remember when I sowed you up on the plane?"

"Vaguely."

"You're gonna need to make a small incision about a centimeter to the left of your graze. Make sure to sterilize the area and the tool-"

"Where-"

"First aid kit. If you don't find one in the master bathroom on the top shelf of the towel closet, check under the sink. If that's still a bust ask one of the maids and insist you want to do it yourself because you don't like being touched by other people."

"You think they'll buy that?"

"I met the prince you're impersonating. He's...eccentric."

Nodding I ask, "What about Daniel's?"

She makes a brief frustrated face. "That's where it gets complicated. His is on the back of his neck. So you're going to have to remove it." My head hangs forward. "He was even harder to kidnap and a little less willing to comply with The Devil's immediate wishes. Nina picked a spot he couldn't easily reach." I lift my head to see where she points to on the back of her neck. "Same thing. A small cut and remove the chip."

"Got it."

"You have to do that before you give him the antidote or there's a chance it won't take properly."

At the end of her sentence, I notice her slightly sway. She shakes away the action, but it doesn't stop me from questioning, "Are you okay? You've looked a little out of it all day."

"I'm fine."

She's lying, but I don't know why. What? I don't know. I don't know if I'll be this skeptical with everything she says, but she just swayed! Something is probably wrong.

"Are you nervous about The Devil? I thought you trusted me."

"I'm fine," she insists again. "I do. Focus. You've got a job to do."

"It's gonna be fun," The Devil invades the conversation and the room. He slides past Mel, his hand touching her side. Instinctively I prepare to lunge when Mel gives me a short shake of her head.

She's right. I know. I know. Can't kill him now. Oh, but it's coming. It's fucking coming.

"You look well for a dying man McCoy," he hums as he slides his hands in his pockets. "That is if you are indeed still dying."

"Still feel like I got hit with a freight train when I woke up this morning, so I'm guessing, yeah," I mouth off. "Now, would you like to check if I began my menstrual cycle too or can we get started?"

"The most redeeming quality about you McCoys is your biggest flaw." With a nod of his head he continues. "Mission is quite simple really. You and your brother are now prince Duke Hastard."

"Hazzard. We're Dukes of Hazzard?"

Fucking seriously?

"Hastard," he corrects with an over enunciation. "You are to each swap the forgery item with the actual one I want. You will arrive ten minutes after your brother in identical clothing on a different bike. This will occur right after valet has a shift change."

"How will we fake that for the cameras?"

"There are no cameras," The Devil answers. "Harrison likes his privacy as much as knowing how much his clients or so called friends do as well. Also, Duke has been invited to many of these parties and declined. Very few people have actually *met* Duke Hastard, so they have no expectations."

I try not smile. "No cameras."

"You'll have an earwig so that I can hear everything every step of the way." He twirls his finger around and the lackey who walked in with him opens the brief case he was holding. "And before you get any clever ideas, I have additional eyes around that party not to mention a GPS tracking device implanted in you."

I drop my jaw just enough to be convincing.

"Oh...you're fuck buddy failed to mention that?" He smirks before looking over Mel who is being gripped harshly by Omar. "Tisk. Tisk. Never know if you can trust that one."

"Obviously not." I growl.

"Aw..." The Devil fakes sympathy. "Feelings hurt?"

I'm gonna put a bullet right through those fucking perfect eyebrows.

"You will swap the sculpture and deliver it back to me. Here. Daniel will deliver the bike to my truck, but also return here with the keys in his hand. It's the only chance you two have at surviving the nasty virus feasting on you."

The lackey leans forward for me to take the sticker sized ear wig.

Merrick used to always bitch about mine being too big. Thank God he never saw these or the bitching would've never ended. You know what, I'd give anything to hear him bitching again.

"Where's the object?"

"Harrison's bedroom. Top floor." The Devil makes another hand motion and the lackey leans forward again. "Use the tools wisely."

I grab the lock picking kit and slip it into my coat jacket pocket. "It's like Christmas."

"Poor people Christmas in deed." His dig has me clamping down on my tongue to hold my composure. "Take your invitation. There's a basic map of the inside of his home in the envelope as well. You're on a time limit."

Because there's not enough fucking pressure breaking into a high class party, pretending to be a prince, and stealing a valuable piece of artwork as well as one of kind motorcycle?

The Devil adjusts his cuffs. "You've got four hours McCoy. Make them count."

"Can I make a request?"

"Serious set of balls," he chortles. "What are you asking for?"

I toss my head at Mel. "The girl."

"I'm gonna kill her McCoy. She's not a trophy you can take home with you."

"I know." Coldly I state, "I just wanna be here when you do. I wanna watch the life drain from her eyes the way she's been watching it drain from mine."

Mel's mouth slides open.

Remind her I'm full of shit please.

"That request I can grant," The Devil says with a pleased tone. "It's fair. Omar, take her to Eden. Tie her up. She can wait there." Mel struggles against Omar, but he simply grips tighter. With a wide smirk he states, "It's been a pleasure Eve. Hopefully your replacement lasts as long as you did."

She chokes out a sob before she's dragged away. My heart thrums so harshly, one wrong breath and it would fall out of me.

Buying her time. That's all I'm doing.

"Your chariot awaits," The Devil smiles once more. "There's GPS wired into your bike. Two addresses. Here and there. Tick tock, McCoy."

**

The ride over was perfect. The combination of the wind, the freedom to move further than the property, and having untouchable horsepower underneath me is rejuvenating.

Now that I've tasted freedom, there's no way I'm ever going back to captivity again. And once Mel is out, I'll let her taste this every chance I get. Trust me. I have a plan.

Getting inside the French style mansion that seems to stretch out for miles was easy enough with the invitation. Valet changed shifts on schedule and I'm smoothly walking around the room with the shoulder bag that contains the forgery. This isn't nerve racking in the least.

Apparently The Devil informed us he was also a photographer. People would assume, that's what was in the bag. I feel like he's lying.

A woman in a slinky red dress wraps her arms around me. "Duke!"

Well hello lady in red....hey just because I'm in love doesn't mean I can't appreciate how hot she looks. Though, her paid for tits and botox face just make me even more thrilled to have a woman with 100% natural beauty.

"Mary Lynn Shivel," she introduces herself, fingers stroking my arm. "Pleasure to finally meet you in person."

Daniel questions, "Room?"

"I bet it is. Drink by the bar?" I try to give my brother information.

"There's one of those on every fucking floor," Daniel grumps.

"I enjoy the blue light of this one, unlike the one on the first floor. This one compliments my eyes."

"Smooth," Daniel chuckles. "Heading up from the service tunnel."

"You do have gorgeous eyes," Mary agrees as we arrive in front of the bar. "A glass of champagne for me."

"And you sir?" The bartender questions.

"You know, I've changed my mind," I state and adjusts the strap on my shoulder.

"Want a clear mind for the night?" She playfully coos. "I don't blame you. I wish I would've had one for my first time..."

Are you getting the feeling The Devil has forgotten to mention something?

Once she has the glass in her hand she turns me to walk back the direction we came. "There's nothing to be nervous about either. Once the masks come on and the clothes come off, it's a very freeing experience."

Whoa...whoa...what?!

Swallowing my nerves, I nod slowly. "I can't wait to see it."

"Good thing you don't have to wait long." Her hand runs up my chest. "I know you prefer men, but hopefully you'll test my waters..."

I smirk. "Maybe. If you'll excuse me, I need to use the restroom."

She let's go of her grip on me just as Daniel starts to grumble, "Did I hear her correctly? We're at a sex party?"

"We're gay at a sex party," I mumble strolling off.

The Devil chuckles to himself but says nothing.

Of course he already fucking knew. One more thing to smile at as he uses us like chess pieces.

"Thought you were using the bathroom." I hear Mary Lynn say to Daniel.

"Don't be seen together," The Devil growls.

"Let us do our job," I defend and peer around the corner.

Daniel instantly spots me.

"You're gonna pay for that attitude McCoy."

"Counting on it," I mutter before mouthing to Daniel. "Meet on the top floor. Ten minutes."

He gives me a nod before saying to Mary, "It was brief. Tell me more about your first time at one of these parties."

Her voice fills the ear pieces, which I hope will act as a distraction to The Devil. The retelling is graphic and filled with so many sexual invitations, if I wasn't focused on saving our asses as well as my loves, I wouldn't mind listening.

It's like hearing porn instead of watching it.

On the top floor I stroll past the open doors, which obviously aren't the bedrooms I'm looking for nor are they big enough to even be considered. At the far end there's a set of closed double doors.

Bingo.

"I've never personally put a banana there," Daniel says in a way that I know he's smiling.

Shaking my head, I slide out my lock picking tools and get to work.

First time I picked a lock? I was six. It was sort of like finding the right block for the right hole as a child. I found something that was similar in flatness, stuck it in the hole, and shimmied it around until the damn thing clicked open. I wanted those cookies, so I got them.

The door clicks open and reveals to me a bedroom fit for a billionaire. The posh décor is more feminine than I would prefer with it's peach tone colors and chocolate browns along with the chandelier. There are frilly pillows and rugs to match.

Is this the master bedroom?

Doubt crowds my thoughts, but only briefly, due to the sound of footsteps. Quickly I slip inside and behind the drapes, making sure to keep my body frozen, and my shoes covered. The footsteps seem light and harmless, but I remain stiff. My fists ball at my sides preparing to swing if necessary. Suddenly there's a light rhythmical tapping. I hone in on it.

You hear it too don't you. It's Living On A Prayer. Go ahead and hum, just do it quietly. Who doesn't love a little Bon Jovi in their life?

Pulling the drape back, I notice Daniel smirking from behind the closed door. He makes a motion for us to speed up the process. My eyes do a scan of the room not spotting the sculpture I'm supposed to be lifting. Frustrated, I start to doubt we're in the right room again.

What? What do you mean turn around?

I glance over my shoulder at the three pieces that are sitting in the wall nook behind a thin curtain closest to the bathroom. With a wide smirk, I hustle over and carefully make the swap.

Uncanny right? See. I'm good at this shit.

Once I've got the pieces switched, I crack open the bathroom door and mouth, "Follow. Me."

Daniel nods and slips inside with me. Behind the closed bathroom door, I start to open the first door looking for the towel closet. Thankful my find is immediate, I search the top shelf for the First Aid kit. The second my hand finds the handle I smile.

See. She can be trusted. Don't wonder how she knows it would be there. Where do you keep yours?

Quietly I place the kit on the table and open my palm. I mouth, "Knife."

He shakes his head.

When my head sarcastically tilts he rolls his eyes and carefully removes it from his jacket pocket. Daniel mouths, "What did you expect?"

I mouth, "That."

"It's awfully quiet," The Devil growls in a displeased tone.

"It's better to be silent when stealing shit than yelling about it," I answer as I pull up my pant leg. "So how about you shut the fuck up, so we can get this done on time?"

The Devil doesn't respond.

I know. I'll pay for that later too.

Sterilizing the knife with one of the wipes in the kit and then sterilizing my fingers, I hand the tool back to my brother, and indicate where he needs to cut. When Daniel shakes his head I mouth, "Cut. Me. We're being tracked." He makes a frustrated face but does as he's told. Carefully he makes a slight slit. I reach inside and pull out the small flashing red device. We work together to get the cut cleaned and bandaged. Afterward Daniel lifts his leg, which is when I shake my head. The puzzled look increases when I point to the back of my neck.

Daniel shakes his head slowly.

I mouth, "Yeah. Turn."

He makes a pissed off expression, but turns around. I clean my hands and the object once more. Even more cautious than he was, I make a small slit where Melody indicated, thankful to see the red flashing device immediately. Removing it slowly, I clean the area and bandage him back up. With both of our GPS trackers wrapped in tissue, we slip them in our pockets. Afterward I grab the shot out of my inside pocket and hand it to him.

"The antidote," I mouth. "Take it now."

He nods and prepares to when there's a set of footsteps headed our direction.

Fuck...

Quickly I grab the first aid kit and slip into the towel closet.

"What are you doing in here?" A voice asks Daniel. "What are you doing in my bathroom?"

Through the crack of the door, I see a man, a man I can only assume is Harrison. Daniel maintains eye contact with him as he answers. "Special guest. Special privileges."

Harrison hums and folds his arms across his chest. "What other special privileges do you feel you should be entitled too?"

I cover my mouth to hold back the laughter.

Daniel's dying inside I just know it.

"Uh..." he stumbles around, clears his throat.

"Don't be nervous Duke. You don't have to share me if you don't want..."

Another urge rips through me to laugh.

My womanizing brother has to pretend to enjoy being hit on by a dude. This is a story I am telling again and again at dinner. You bet your ass I am.

Daniel's eyes meet me through the crack of the door.

"You can do anything to me you want," Harrison insists. "Anything."

"Oh yeah?" Daniel questions. "Anything at all?"

"Dom me," he begs relentlessly.

You know, you see this kind of shit in porn, well I've seen the male, female version of it, and you think it doesn't really happen. But here we are. At an entire party apparently devoted to it.

"Get on your knees. Place your hands behind your back. Close your eyes."

"Yes master," Harrison whimpers and drops to his knees.

Once his eyes are closed Daniel makes a hand motion for me to exit. "Keep them closed."

"Yes master."

I slip out of the door and quietly out of the bathroom while Daniel shakes his head at me. With a crooked smirk I give him a wink.

He mouths. "Fuck you."

Making the motion like Harrison's going to suck his cock, I silently laugh.

What'd you expect? Me to have no fun? You've met us right?

"Daniel," The Devil's voice invades my ears. "Where are you?"

"Heading to make the swap now," I lie for my brother, grateful it's hard to tell even our voices apart.

"Good. The rig is in place."

"Still searching for the sculpture," Daniel leaks into the conversation. "It's not on display as expected."

"Asshole probably hid it in case anyone got curious during the party," The Devil mumbles. "Find my fucking statue."

"Yeah," Daniel answers just steps behind me.

"Drew speed it up. You need to follow Daniel to the drop off point, so he can follow you back here. I want both of you putting objects into my hands."

"Got it," we answer in unison.

The two of us head in opposite directions, the end result needing to be the same. I arrive near the elevators which is when Daniel mouths, "Switch tags."

Nodding, I tuck it into my coat jacket and head into the elevator. On a deep breath I prepare for the elementary school easy swap. I stroll out of the elevator to see one of the security guards as well as one of the valet boys.

"Sir," the young man calls to me. "You didn't want me to bring your vehicle up for you?"

"No," I calmly answer. "Harrison told me I could admire his bike before I left. Didn't feel the need to have you bring mine all the way up when I could kill two birds with one stone."

"Wise choice," the valet replies. "His bike is this direction..." While strolling beside him I spot my brother's bike a few spaces over from mine. "We just ask no one touches it."

"Of course not," I agree. Beside my brother's bike, I abruptly stop. "One moment. I need to tie my shoe." Leaning down I notice the security guard glance away giving me the smallest chance to pull the tag off.

"Mr. Smith likes to display his collective pieces next to everyone else's. He likes the way it makes everyone look beneath him." The valet stops in front of the legendary motorcycle. "Here we are."

I suppress my urge to look impressed. With a hum, I nod slowly and stroll around the bike, eyes fixated on the spot I need to drop the tag.

Believe me, I wanna drool over this baby. I want to touch her in ways that could make the most experienced bike rider fall to his knees. I want to take her away from this display prison she's stuck in and free her. Yeah. Just like I wanna free Mel.

With my arms folded, I continue to stare waiting for the expected cue. The security guard gets a page that causes him to shift uncomfortably. Out of the corner of my eyes, I wait until the guard makes a hand motion for the valet to come to his side. He hesitates to leave me. The guard makes another hand motion while glancing at his phone once more. At that moment I slip the tag on and move my body to be beside the valet.

"Do I need to end my admiration early?"

He starts to bounce on the balls of his feet. When the security guard looks up he sighs, "Yes. I'm sorry sir. I need to get to your vehicle. Ticket please." I hand it to him and we start to move across the garage. Calling out to the guard he announces, "I'll be right there."

The two of us arrive at my motorcycle. He scurries away to grab my keys. I keep my eyes on my bike. The Valet hands me my keys, politely thanks me for being a guest, and wishes me safe travels. On the bike, I secure my bag, the sound of feet moving faster, grabbing my attention. The guard and the valet move together, both with panicked expressions. Making a smooth exit out of the garage and out the gate, I pull onto a side road close by to wait for my brother.

Impatiently I tap my foot.

What's taking him so long? This shit should've went by quick and smooth. Get the guard out, get a spare newer, unfamiliar with the place Valet to retrieve the vehicle. Get the fuck out....what's the hold up?

More time passes by and my nerves grow restless. Suddenly there's shouting over my earpiece. "We've got a problem!"

Baffled by his loud exclamation, I snap back, "What kind of problem?"

"A red and blue problem!" He screams, voice still in a panic. "And it's on my ass!"

Before I can ask his location or a heads up of where to meet him, he races by, flashing cop lights following.

"Fuck!"

"We're gonna need a little extra time," Daniel calls to The Devil. Without waiting for him to answer, he gripes, "Thought you had called the dogs off!"

"I did," The Devil growls. "That is not one of mine."

"Well we don't have any!" Daniel's voice gets louder. "Triple D where the fuck are you?"

I start the bike up. "Where do you want me to be?"

"I took the side road, first right!" Daniel rushes out. "Drop point is off the highway, exit 679. Abandoned warehouse parking lot. Help me get there!"

"On it!" Increasing the speed of my bike, I take the route we came with the idea of hopping back onto the highway a little later. Flying down the two lane curvy rode, I accelerate until I'm pushing speeds that will grab the cops attention if he hasn't called in for back up yet.

Zooming onto the highway it doesn't take long to spot him or the cop that's riding his ass.

"Right lane." I announce. "Fall back."

"Are you fucking serious?" Daniel grumbles.

"Do it."

I push my speed and come around on the right side, revving to grab the cops attention. When he spots me, I fly forward, the intention for him to leave Daniel to come after me.

"Falling off," Daniel informs. "Three more exits and you've made it. Lose him before that!"

"Don't you get caught," The Devil grumbles into the ear piece. "Don't. You. Dare. Get. Caught."

Easy for him to say. He's not the one with a cop so far up his ass, he can taste the doughnut the dude had on his break.

The cop is tight on me as I weave around traffic, and for the first time I'm afraid I might not make it out of this one. Suddenly there's another cop with his lights on, waiting to assist. Between the two, I realize I'm fucked. The best I can do is get off the highway and try a possible Shake and Bake.

While they are running my plates before they take my keys, run off again. You'd be surprised how often that actually works.

I pull off at the exit like planned.

Who knows. Maybe The Devil's man is packing heat and can help. Fuck, maybe Daniel can too.

"I see you," Daniel announces.

"You see my visitors?"

Daniel sighs, "Yeah. I've got a plan. Pull over."

Gliding off to the side of the road, the cops follow.

The Devil repeats, "I warned you McCoys."

After I kill my engine, I leave the keys in, but lift my hands slowly. "Middle Man, Shake and Bake?"

"Even better."

The two cops get off their bikes, weapons drawn and yell, "On the ground! Now!"

With a deep sigh, I start to follow the instructions, which is when one of them yells, "Slowly! Keep those hands where we can see them!"

Lowering myself onto the ground, I let my knees hit the concrete, the fabric of the designer suit providing no cushion.

Stupid fucking suit.

"All the way down!" One of the cops yells as he continues to approach.

The Devil snaps, "Bring me my statue no matter the cost. Am I clear?"

"Crystal," I whisper back.

A pair of black boots appear in front of my face. With my heart thrumming against the road, I try to lay still. Suddenly a pair of hands roughly searches me quickly, before I'm being yanked upward. As soon as I'm on my feet my jaw drops to where I just was.

No fucking way...

The cop motions to his lip and then to my ear. Next he motions what he wants me to do with it. I reach in my ear and remove the communication device. After placing it with the GPS tracking device I leave them both on the ground next to the wheel of my motorcycle.

Once everything is there and we're a good distance from it, I prepare to say something, which is when I receive the finger to the lips motion again. We approach the parking lot where the big rig is already loaded. Stealthy the two people dressed in cop uniforms each move to the driver's door. I give Daniel a glance who is smirking while he smokes his cigarette.

Yeah, but he's always smoked. Started about the same time he could drive himself to grab a pack.

Before I can say anything to him, I hear the vehicle door open, and a heavy sigh. "Really, Madden? You didn't think I could handle knocking the guy out?"

A giant smile comes from me as Knox pushes him out of her way. "I didn't want you to knock him out."

"Why? Afraid she'd break a nail?" Daniel calls out with a laugh.

"Keep talkin' shit and see how many I break on you," she storms over with Madden at her side.

"He made the call that he had the package, so as far as The Devil is concerned this is already in route," Daniel announces. "We've got a noise scrambler. He'll think there's a scuffle, shots fired, and then it'll be silent."

Destin tosses an arm around my shoulder. "It's so fucking good to see you, bro."

Turning the half ass hug into a full one, I give him a heavy pat. "Fuck, man. I missed you."

"Yeah," he replies pulling away.

"Save the sentimental moments to be shared over milk and cookies," Knox snaps. "We've gotta get this moving before The Devil gets any clue what's happening."

"How is any of this possible?" Looking at Destin I ask, "The Devil is watching you."

"He is watching us," Destin gleefully says. When I tilt my head, he explains, "We pre- recorded video footage, had it synced, and chopped as necessary. There is enough pre- recorded answers to conversations to get us by."

"You would need someone looped into his live video and feeding him the appropriate answers-"

"It's a good thing Vinnie was accepting favors," Destin's response gets a nod of approval from me.

"Like my plan?" Daniel gloats.

"Your plan?" Knox snips.

"This was so my fucking plan!" Daniel snaps.

"Part of it!"

"How'd you get this shit set up?"

"You weren't the only one who had a girl on his dick willing to grant him a favor."

Hearing him talk about Mel like that balls my fist.

I know. Not the ideal time for this fucking fight, but I don't enjoy hearing anyone talk about her like that.

"One of the nights Nina and I were fucking, I managed to get a hold of her phone while she was out and send a game plan message."

I wonder if we have to save her too...

Impressed I ask, "How'd you get the final call to them?"

"You'd be surprised what a guy who wants to touch your dick is willing to do for you, including letting you use his untraceable phone to make a brief phone call."

"Proud of that?" Knox teases. When Daniel glares she adds, "You play a convincing gay Dom."

"Can we please focus?" Madden invades the conversation. "The clock is running. Knox, are you sure you can drive this thing?"

"Are you questioning how much power I can handle between my legs?"

Madden grits his teeth.

And their sexual tension moments make an appearance.

Daniel chuckles and puts out his cigarette. "Come on Mad Man. What did you expect?"

Madden grouses, "I swear when we get home..."

"Yeah, yeah," Daniel brushes him off. He extends his hand at Destin. "Keys."

Destin drops a key into his hand. Skeptical Daniel looks up at him. "You think these will work?"

"Well enough to get your ass out of there," Madden invades the conversation. "Give him the keys. By the time he can get them to where he believes his new long lost treasure is, Mr. Harrison will be changing more than just the locks on all his doors."

"Man, I can't believe we have to give this back to him," Daniel whines.

I lift my eyebrows. "So we're giving it back to him?"

"*We're* not," Destin corrects. "The cops are."

"We're turning it into the cops?" I croak.

"The Commissioner," Madden informs on a sigh. "And we aren't. We're leaving it in Vinnie's garage then an anonymous tip. As far as that sculpture you're gonna let him take it."

"With an addition made," Destin points out. He pulls something small out of his pocket. "Slip this in the most inconspicuous spot you can find. It's a tracking device. We can use it to pin point the different places of The Devil's location. Start watching him the way he watches us."

"You don't think he'll be suspicious?" I question. "What happens if he gives it to a buyer?"

"He won't," Madden assures. "He likes that kinda shit too much."

"You ready?" Daniel asks grabbing something out of Knox's hands.

"Yeah," I sigh. "Did you take the shot?"

"Yep."

Knox hands me a knife as well. Looking up I question, "No guns?"

Madden shakes his head. "The Devil has cut us out and has an eye on everything and everyone we usually turn too. No vests either."

"In other words, don't go in like John Wayne," Knox scolds.

"Yee-haw," Daniel says before turning his fingers into guns.

Idiot...but fuck, I've missed him.

"No yee-haw." Madden points. "Both of you get your asses home safe."

I nod, the microdot still on my finger. Heading back the way I came, Daniel calls to me from the spare bike he was brought by the eighteen wheeler. "When you get on, follow my lead."

Hustling back down the street, I slip the dot on the statue where I don't think it can be found. Afterward, I slide the GPS back in my pocket and the ear wig back in my ear.

There's heavy breathing before Daniel's voice huffs, "Cops are down."

Breathing hard I state, "We're on our way."

There's a long pause before The Devil questions, "My statue?"

"On me."

"Do not make me wait any longer," he snips.

When we arrive at the cottage, there's two large black SUVs parked out front. We park across the road beside some trees knowing there's a possibility we're going to need a fast escape when it all goes south.

Yep. I said when. Not if. This is not going to be smooth by any means.

Passing by the SUVs, we're startled when the driver's door pops open. Instinctively Daniel prepares to grab his knife, but I stop him with a hard clamp on the shoulder. Omar gives us both a long hard look.

You get the feeling this isn't going to be good?

"Bag and keys," Omar demands.

Daniel rushes to say, "The Devil said-"

"Oh right," The Devil chimes in on the ear wig. "Sorry McCoys that I can't be there to receive my rewards personally, but Omar will bring them to me without an issue."

"Hand them over," Omar commands, this time with a harsher tone.

On a sigh I shove the bag at his chest before Daniel drops the keys in his hand.

"The antidote?" I question eyes still watching Omar as he loads the objects into the vehicle.

"I am a man of my word," he states. "It's inside. Two shots. Waiting for you on the coffee table. Feel better you two." The evilness in his tone is followed by a small snigger. "Oh and your one request, Drew? She's waiting for you to give her a dose of her own medicine..."

There's another cold chuckle and silence. We wait for a moment for more information. To further be taunted. When it's obvious that he's not coming back, we pull the ear pieces out and step on them.

At that moment, Omar shuts the car door and takes a step towards us. Seeing Daniel prepared to attack if necessary, I decide it's best to take a similar stance. "McCoy, do you really want Melody dead?"

For the first time since we've met I see a flash of concern on his face. It doesn't look like it's for show. It doesn't look like it's another test from The Devil. No this shit looks real. Like...he cares about her.

What do you mean he does? How would you know?

I swallow the urge to tell him the truth. "Why?"

"Answer me," he growls. "Do. You. Want. Her. Dead?"

My lips press together. Slowly I shake my head.

"Are you gonna save her?"

"I sure the fuck am."

"Good. I didn't buy that bullshit betrayal act, but neither did The Devil," he informs me. "There are two men standing watch outside Eden and one inside with her. He plans to have them put a bullet in her head right after yours."

Immediately I argue, "I thought-"

"You thought wrong," Omar corrects. "When he got wind to the idea of Melody fucking you, he decided not to let you two live any longer than necessary." In a hushed tone advises, "There are four men waiting inside to kill you. Your best shot is to go around back, take out those protecting Melody, and use their weapons on the ones inside. If you don't go inside at all The Devil will suspect something and this whole experience will feel like child's play. Save her. Kill them. Leave no witnesses."

As he takes a couple steps back, Daniel questions, "Why are you telling us this?"

"Because there's nothing I can do to protect her," he confesses, eyes still on me. "But you McCoys can."

He climbs in the SUV without another word, leaving us alone in the front yard to devise a very quick plan. The two of us watch him start to pull away, which we know will be the indicator not only have we arrived, but to expect us at any moment.

You're damn right it's gonna be tricky, but hey! That's what McCoys are.

Melody

My eyes roll around in my head desperate to stay open, but I know I don't have long left.

It's alright. I planned it this way.

A groan comes from me and Rex sighs, "Why couldn't you have just been a good girl, Melody?"

Not responding to his stupid question, I simply let out another moan of discomfort as my head bobbles around.

"You just had to fuck McCoy," his rant continues. "I knew I should've just fucked you like I wanted. Taken what I wanted. What was mine."

"She was never yours," Drew's voice joins the conversation.

As best as I can I open my eyes, so grateful to see him.

That is really him right? Am I seeing things?

With his gun cocked he slowly approaches Rex whose gun is already pressed against my temple. "Now get that shit away from my girl."

"Your girl?" Rex barks.

It's so heavy. My head is so fucking heavy now...

"You know what, McCoy? I'm gonna fucking kill you. Fuck her. Then kill her." Rex describes, the weapon finally not against my skull.

Through slightly closed eyes, I can see Drew's cocky smile.

Now doesn't seem like a good time for that.

Suddenly a buzzing noise speeds by forcing my eyes open seconds before Rex falls over, the gun dropping from his clutches. Turning my head the best I can, I watch as Drew lifts his own weapon and pulls the trigger. The shot pierces Rex's skull.

Before I can even try to comment, another voice says, "A head shot? Really? What are we in Grand Theft Auto?"

"We've been living Grand Theft Auto from birth," Drew replies back, his hands starting to untie the ropes.

At least I think that's what happening. Everything is so blurry...

"Still..."

"No. Witnesses," Drew says catching my limp body as it prepares to fall over. "Mel baby," he calls to me, his warm hand on my face. "Look at me...come on baby, look at me."

I do my best to make eye contact with him.

His thumb strokes my cheek. "There are those gorgeous blues I love."

"Well if you wanna keep seeing them, I suggest we get to moving," the other voice snaps.

With all the energy I have I look up to see the face that's been speaking.

Okay...am I seeing double? What? Right! They're Triplets!

"D-D-Daniel?"

He wiggles his eyebrows at me. "The one and only."

"Don't hit on my girl."

"I was being friendly."

"Don't be *that* kind of friendly!"

"Now?" Daniel snaps. "You wanna do this now?"

I'm with Daniel on that. We can fuss over his overly friendly tone later.

A howl of displeasure frees itself from me again.

"Can you walk?" Drew touches my cheek once more, which drags my eyes back to his. A small shrug comes from me. "I need you to try, okay?"

I give him a nod and try to rise to my feet. Within seconds my knees buckle. All of sudden there are two sets of arms around me, helping my failing body.

"Let's leave her here until-"

"No fucking way," Drew growls beside me.

"Well we can't carry her and shoot the place the fuck up. I'm not a physics major, but I've seen enough action movies to know that shit can't work. We have to leave her somewhere, Drew."

There's a small silence as we continue to move forward.

At least I think we're moving forward.

"I know a safe spot," Drew sighs. "Over there."

Thankfully I'm carried not too far or long. Helplessly I'm laid down on the ground in a spot I know very well, even with the way I'm feeling now.

"You're sure about this?" A voice, I'm assuming is Daniel's asks.

They even sound alike when they are this close together. Or is that cause of what's in my system?

"Yeah. The cameras can't see her." Drew's face appears in front mine. "I won't leave without you, baby. I promise."

A single nod comes from me.

I hear the sounds of weapons being checked before my eyes watch two sets of feet go through the sliding glass door. Doing my best to keep my falling eyes open, I watch as commotion ensues. The ringing of gun shots which should sound deafening are no louder than a small humming of a child. Unsure how many more breaths I have like this I make one final attempt to spot Drew. Unexpectedly the fire fight falls back into the kitchen. A body falls to the ground obviously hit. I struggle to move, to get a better idea, any single clue if it was one of The Devil's men or one of the McCoys. Just as I take one last conscious breath, I catch a glimpse of the injured face.

My mouth drops to scream no, but instead darkness takes me.

Melody

You know when you're having a nightmare and you try to wake yourself up? Don't you hate when you can't? Don't you hate when you wiggle and shift, violently tossing your body around in hopes of prying yourself from the clutches of the demons holding you down in dream world? What? What do you mean just open my eyes? They won't open! I tried! I tried! Help...help please. Okay. Fine. One more time I'll try.

My eye lids try to shift open, but seem to stop before finishing the action. However my ears can hear the steady sound of a machine and the low murmur of voices.

Can you hear them too? Are those real or just in my head?

"She's not even awake yet," a female voice sighs.

"Well, like the rest of you I have time to wait," an authoritative male voice states in return.

"You could wait outside," another suggests.

"Or in here. Right where I am."

Frustrated, I use all the energy I have to push my eyelids open to see a room filled with slightly familiar faces. It takes a moment for my eyes to adjust, but once they do the faces surrounding me actually fill me with comfort.

"Oh look," the only face that doesn't bring me comfort starts. "She's awake."

"Can't you give her a moment?" The female, I assume is Knox, asks.

He gives her a head shake. "No." Suddenly his face is turned towards me and he steps forward, "Melody Porter?"

Clearing my throat I answer, "Yes, Commissioner."

"Welcome back to the world of the living."

The Commissioner is just as scary in person as he is in photos. He's got the build of an old boxer, toffee colored skin, a bald head, and a beard. Of course I know his face. How could I not? The Devil's obsessed with avoiding him as much as he is with taunting him. His face is one of the first you learn when you tangle with the man downstairs.

"The McCoys have been kind enough to watch over you, claiming you as a family member," he describes something that makes me wanna pull my eyes out of his dark ones to thank them. But I don't. I don't even take an extra breath. "Awfully kind of them, don't you think?" When I nod he asks, "What can you tell me about your employer?"

I know I shouldn't protect him, but not protecting him could possibly stop protecting myself if I'm not careful. "Excuse me?"

"You work for The Devil don't you?"

My lips press together in refusal to answer.

Unexpectedly the door cracks open and a nurse's face appears. She's a slightly older woman with a worn out expression on her face. "You're awake, Miss Porter."

"I am."

"That's a surprise," she says softly. "I'll be back in just a few to clear the room and check your vitals, alright?"

Once I nod, she shuts the door quietly, but no one else objects to the idea of being escorted out.

And I mean no one. Guess I deserve that for getting him killed....God. I can't believe it...

He shoves his hands in his pockets. "Do you need me to repeat the question?"

"I think I might want a lawyer before I answer the question," my scratchy voice sighs before sniffling away the tears.

"I understand." The Commissioner nods. Casually he turns over his shoulder and motions for the other officer in the room to come beside him. He whispers something in his ear and pulls back. "Don't forget. Two sugars."

"Yes, Commissioner," he agrees before dismissing himself.

As soon as he's gone The Commissioner pulls a pair of cuffs from his pocket.

Nervously I ask, "Wh-wha-what are those for?"

"For you," his answer is nonchalant. "You want a lawyer, now's the part where I read you your rights and tell yu what you say can and will be used against you in the court of law." When my mouth cracks open it immediately begins to wobble. I can see a movement out of the corner of my eye, but it's stopped abruptly. "Look, we can handle this one of two ways. I can cuff you. Read your rights. Arrest you for suspicion to commit kidnapping. Kidnapping. Suspicion to commitment murder on multiple accounts. Attempted murder on multiple accounts. Get you in the system. Behind bars where The Devil, who I'm pretty sure wanted you dead, can then once again get you that way. Get you in front of a judge, a courtroom, who even if they declare you innocent, which they won't, would then put you right at the top of The Devil's hit list. Should I continue or is my picture crisp enough?"

In a meek voice I answer, "Very clear, sir."

"Good," he sighs. "Because personally I like option two better."

"Which is?"

"I keep you alive. You answer any and all questions about The Devil, his business, and associates. You do this, we strike a deal to count all your corroborating information and testimony as time served. You never set foot in a cell or even the precinct."

That sounds like a hell of a deal doesn't it?

"And just so you know I am a man of my word. You know The Devil's reach, but in case you may have under estimated it, the nurse that should've been back by now, was just arrested by my officer who you thought left to get me coffee."

There's a sharp gasp in the room to match my own.

Was that you?

"On The Devil's payroll. Most likely with instructions to kill you if you actually woke up." The information causes me to shift uncomfortably again. "Now, which option would you like to take Miss Porter?"

Scary in a different way from The Devil, but still scary, right?

Without hesitating I reply, "Anything you wanna know."

"Good. Let's start." He shoves the cuffs back in his pocket. "Do you know anything about the whereabouts of Prince Duke Hastard?"

"He was drugged and put on a plane. Currently he's staying at a hotel in Belize being kept by one of The Devil's babysitters. He's being heavily sedated with memory suppressors. When you do get to him there's a high chance he won't remember anything after a few weeks ago."

The information receives a slow nod. "And how do you know that?"

"I am, well, was, The Devil's pharmacist."

"Meaning?"

"I um...I was in charge of helping create healing agents, hallucinogens, as well as various poisons which aided in his torture tactics."

Why am I still alive? Do you hear what I've done for the last few years of my life? I deserve to be the one on the ground with my eyes wide open. Not him...not him.

"Were you the female that helped keep my daughter drugged?"

My mouth trembles, but I confess, "Yes."

"Were you the female that kept her taken and alive?"

I whisper once more. "Yes."

To my surprise he quietly says, "Thank you." When my eyebrows lift in shock he adds, "She says she remembers you trying to help not hurt her. Thank you."

Unsure of what to say I simply nod.

The Commissioner changes gears back to his original line of questioning. "Were you partially responsible for helping kidnap Drew and Daniel McCoy?"

Quietly I answer, "Yes."

"She's also the one who helped heal them," the female voice pipes in. "Give her credit for that too."

He raises his hand. "I will, Knoxie. No need to worry."

"I wasn't worried."

She's just as protective as Drew mentioned. I wonder how much she's going to hate me soon.

"Do you have any idea where The Devil is now?"

"Can you charge him with something this very moment?" I counter. When he tilts his head at me in question, I sigh, "You fight straight ahead Commissioner. Rarely does he. I know you've been cleaning out the system, ridding it of those under his thumb, but he still has a few major players in place, so unless you have concrete evidence prepared by someone who is not Danielle Tambert, you will be wasting your time and showing him more cards than he needs to see. The way he's acting now, the way you've got him feeling is like a wounded animal trapped in a corner. Don't lose that."

To my surprise he smiles. "Exactly how I want him feeling. And yes, DA Danielle Tambert has been removed and began singing what she knows herself about The Devil."

Turns out The Commissioner really is making progress. Good. The Devil needs a reason to stay scared.

"We actually have his fingerprints all over a stolen item that was recently stolen from Harrison Delmont."

How did....How did Drew get those?

"Thankfully the item was returned, but Mr. Delmont would like to press charges-"

"You may want to inform Mr. Delmont to stay away from his priceless statue of 'Skon'. It's a forgery that contains two active toxic agents that when breathed constantly over several days will damage your nervous system eventually resulting in a full shut down."

Yeah. That's what we had him replace it with. See. The Devil is always trying to cover his tracks or make someone pay for something.

After a long stare of disbelief of the information he says, "Will do immediately. With Mr. Delmont wanting to press charges for theft and now attempted murder, I think it is safe to say we have a couple balls rolling. Any information you can provide about The Devil's whereabouts is crucial."

Rubbing my throbbing head I answer, "He was last headed for his beach resort on the east coast of the state. It's not in his name. His homes are listed under aliases. I don't know them."

"General area?"

"Private beach on Vanlovua."

A long exhale comes from me, which prompts someone to voice, "Can the rest of this wait? Look at her. She clearly needs more rest."

The Commissioner gives me a hard look and a nod. "Rest."

"What about her safety?" Knox chimes in harshly. "What's your plan to protect her?"

"I plan to let The Devil think she's dead," he quickly answers.

"And put her where?" The strong voice asks, but I don't let my eyes shift that direction.

I can't face the remaining McCoys. Not yet.

"WITSEC if she would like." He pauses before adding, "However, if I know anything about McCoy men, you do one helluva job protecting the people you call family. Better than any marshal ever could. Choice is hers." His eyes fall to me. "I'll give you a couple hours to decide if you want a spot in the program or if you would rather remain dead in the care of the McCoys, which we will then need to discuss what that entails."

"Got it," the strong voice declares. "We will speak soon, Commissioner."

"Miss Porter," he says with his eyes in mine. "I'll be back this evening."

Without further discussion he turns and heads out of the room. As soon as the door shuts so do my eyes.

I don't wanna be in WITSEC. But maybe it wouldn't be so bad to get a fresh start? A new identity? But can I do that?

"How do you feel?" A voice I know lifts my eyes up.

"A little worn out, but I'll be fine. I drugged myself, so I knew the consequences."

"That takes balls," Knoxie quickly insists, folding her arms across her chest.

Madden, which I know because he's the only one who doesn't look like the triplets snaps, "Knox."

"What?" She gives him a harsh glare. "The rest of you can barely bandage your knuckles without crying like a bitch."

Her attitude causes me to giggle a little, which prevents me from getting swept away in how gorgeous she is.

Bikini model body with a biker mouth? How does anyone compete with that?

The two remaining McCoy triplets are at the foot of my bed with their arms folded across their chests.

It's insane how identical they look side by side. Same clothing. Same expressions. The differences are so subtle that if I hadn't spent almost two weeks staring into a specific pair of eyes, I wouldn't know the difference in the one who died.

Trying to ease some of the tension in my body I shift. "You three really look...just...like photocopied versions of one another."

In unison they ask, "Can you tell us apart?"

My eyes oscillate back and forth, but I say nothing.

"You love one of us," the one on the left comments.

"Or so you say," the one on the right adds.

"Which one is which?" Their questioning in tandem makes me tense.

Nothing like being accused of not knowing the only person you love more than yourself.

I point to the one on the left. "Come here, please."

Neither make an expression to give me a hint if I'm right or not. Instead he strolls over and leans for me to speak in his ear. After a few quick words, I place my hand on his face, and he nods. I then motion for the other to come over. When he arrives on the other side of me, he leans forward just as the one to the left had.

The moment he's close enough I slap him across the face.

You're damn right I did!

"Ou!" He screeches.

"How fucking dare you imply I don't know the man I love when I see him," I sharply snap. His mouth bobs, but I don't let him speak. "I risked my life for you! I was ready to die Drew McCoy so you could live! You told me to trust you when you couldn't even trust that I would know who you were!"

"I knew I liked her," Knox whispers.

"You didn't trust me!" Drew shouts back. "If you trusted me you would've believed me when I said I would come back for you!"

"I did!"

"Then why'd you try to kill yourself!"

"I didn't!" The shrieking continues. "I took enough to knock myself unconscious. I knew you and your brothers had some sort of plan. You would need more time than The Devil was going to allow. I gave myself enough to make sure I would stay passed out until you could get me somewhere safe. It also allowed for worst case scenario, which was him killing you before you stepped back on the property, to have my fail safe in place."

"I don't even know what that means," Drew sighs.

"It means, had you not gotten me to a hospital, had I still been stuck with The Devil, and he chose not to put a bullet in my brain, phase 2 of the mixture I took would've set in. It was a two phase drug. First phase unconsciousness. Checking my vitals at a hospital they would've spotted my system needed to be flushed ridding my body of the second drug which would have killed me once the first one wore off."

"Basically she made it so if you didn't save her, she didn't have to live without you," Knox explains.

That's what I said isn't it?

Drew slips his hand with mine and presses his forehead against mine. "Oh Mel..."

Tears start to sting the sides of my eyes. In a whimper, I cry, "I'm sorry, Drew. I'm sorry about Daniel."

Hearing his brother's name causes his own tears to tumble from him. He doesn't say anything as he wraps himself around me. I hold him tightly to my body, eyes shut. The entire room is filled with so much strain it's suffocating.

After a moment he pulls away and I shake my head. "It's all my fault. If you hadn't come back for me-"

"No," Drew stops me. Wiping away his tears with the back of his hand he shakes his head. "Don't."

"But-"

"You didn't shoot him in the lung," Drew states. The information raises my eyebrows. "And you didn't dive in front of a bullet to save me." My hand catches my gasp. With a trembling voice he says, "I tried to save him. I drove as fast as I could." His eyes lift to his brothers. "I did. I held his hand when he told me to...." Tears congregate once more. "That was it. When Daniel made me reach for his hand, I knew it was too late..." Finally he looks back down at me. "He was...DOA."

"You should've never come back for me," I whisper my guilt.

"If you wouldn't have been there to save them, they'd both be dead," Madden's declaration turns my face.

"They had the antidote already," I argue.

"We did," Drew agrees. "But The Devil was expecting us to walk through the front door, which without you alive, we would have. We would've walked into our own massacre. Omar gave us a fighting chance because of *you*. He wanted you saved as much as I did."

Omar...Geez, what's The Devil going to do if he finds out Omar helped them? Pray for him please. Pray that The Commissioner finds The Devil before he can do anything to the only other man who risked his life to save mine.

A hush falls across the room. It's at that moment I look up and around at the faces that are stained with tears. Destin and Drew who in pain look remarkably different. Destin's face looks soft, sweet, and in desperation of saving. Drew's looks hardened, hurt, and trying to explode into an uncontrollable rage. It's similar to the grim one on Madden's face. Knoxie looks beautiful even as tears fall from her eyes silently. The sight of these people who've just lost a family member I couldn't help save hurts my own heart to the point my chest starts to constrict.

I didn't deserve to live. He did. Yet here I am. I can't undo that. I can't replace my life for his. I swear, if I could, I would. What can I do? Well...yeah...I guess I can do that. I can take care of Drew the best I can. I swear to you and Daniel both, I'll do everything I can to keep him alive and them from losing one more McCoy.

Drew

Leaning against my bike, which part of me now loathes, I stare off into the cloudy distance.

"I'm so fucking tired of going to the graveyard," Destin mutters from beside me.

"We all are," I reply softly, eyes still focused ahead. "We all fucking are, bro."

He sniffles and sighs, "I don't think I can do this, Drew. I can't put Middle Man in the ground."

My face finally falls.

I have to bury another brother today. I have to fucking say goodbye again. No one told him to dive in front of that fucking bullet for me. He should be standing here mourning me. He should be here against this bike, cursing my name and smoking a cigarette. You know what that bastard said when I asked him why he did that? You know what he fucking said? That he owed me. That he owed me for saving his ass his entire life. That it was about time he could save mine. If that shit wasn't fucking enough, he had the fucking nerve to say he owed Mel one for saving his life long enough to see his brothers one final time. Fuck him for that. Fuck him for all of that! He's a smartass asshole! No, I can't stop crying. You stop crying. Fuck. And no, I didn't tell my brothers he said that, just Mel. She deserved to know. She cried harder when I did. Apparently survivor's guilt is real shit.

"I can't..."

Turning my voice to him, but keeping my face down I state, "We don't have a choice." The back of my hand rubs my nose before I lift my eyes back to his. "We bury our brother. We send him off with love then we don't stop until we make sure The Devil gets acquainted with the same six feet he made Daniel and Merrick meet."

Destin nods and shoves his hands in his pockets.

That's a fucking promise if I've ever made one.

"Hey," Mel's soft voice joins us. "I'm...ready."

My eyes glance over the black form fitting dress Knox let her borrow. The sight of all of her curves on display makes my dick twitch in my jeans.

Of all the fucking times...

She leans up and plants a soft kiss on my cheek. In a whisper she says, "Knoxie warned me you would react that way."

A small smile twitches on my face. "You ready for your first ride?"

Her eyes widen.

Yeah, can you believe it? Been home about a week and haven't taken my bike out yet. Partially because we've barely left the apartment other than to meet with The Commissioner, who is charging The Devil with kidnapping me and Daniel's murder among other things, and partially because I didn't have the heart too.

I hand her a helmet before I crawl on my bike and start it almost in unison with Destin. Once we're both settled, I offer her a hand to hop on, insisting, "Hold on tight."

Destin pulls out first, with me tightly behind. Melody immediately wraps herself tighter around me. Increasing the speed, I find the freedom in flying down the road I once used to. As we agreed before we started the journey to Aunt Kelli's, we take the long route, giving our own silent solute to Daniel. On curves we rev up to speeds that would easily scare anyone, but are ones we both know are where we are most comfortable. While on straight aways we lean a little harsher to each side than necessary.

We arrive in front of our Aunt Kelli's home in the middle nowhere.

Growing up, after our mom died we lived with Aunt Kelli and Uncle D for a while. Uncle D taught me how to ride my first motorcycle. It was his lifestyle. Dad was for cars, but us, all three of us triplets, had a calling for motorcycles.

I hang my helmet on one of the bars while Mel places her on the seat. As soon as her head is free she tosses her long hair around.

She refuses to keep it braided like she used to. Says that part of her is dead. She wanted to cut it, but I vetoed that shit. I wanna keep pulling it during sex. There's something about wrapping my hand around it while I tug her towards me, I can't get enough of.

"Scared?"

"With you?" Mel smirks. "Never..."

I offer her my hand. Once she takes it, I lead her away from Aunt Kelli's house towards the McCoy junk yard. Strolling behind Destin, I drop her hand and wrap my arm around her shoulder. Melody looks around at the junk yard that used to belong to Uncle D that Madden's now responsible for.

Dad had the mechanic shop. Uncle D had this place. They always had a way of completing each other the way brothers should. The way the three of us always did.

Behind the junkyard is where the McCoy cemetery is. Under a large shaded area created by two trees there are two rows of tombstones. Dad and Uncle D's are beside each other's, while Ben's is behind his fathers and my mother as well as Merrick is behind my dad's.

That's where we're about to put Daniel.

As if hearing my thoughts, Mel slips her arm around me, pulling me in tightly. I welcome the support as we come to a stop between Madden and Destin. On the other side of him is Vinnie with his two girlfriends Shelby and Krissy. Next to them is where my Aunt Kelli is, Knox holding her up for support.

She's helped bury the most McCoys out of all of us. How any person doesn't just throw in the towel after burying not only your husband but your only son is beyond me. Sometimes I wonder how Aunt Kelli stays as strong as she has for all these years. I swear...she's gonna crack at any minute.

Madden who has the shovel in one hand and Daniel's ashes in an old oil can in the other, doesn't even look up as he hands it to me. Instead he keeps his eyes pasted on the hole we have to put Middle Man in.

Fuck...I don't know how I'm supposed to do this.

Knowing I have to speak first I open my mouth to try. Not a sound comes out. I'm not even sure I'm still breathing on my own. With the steadiest clutch I can maintain, I stare at the can containing the remains of my brother.

Destin's not alone. He's not the only one who can't fucking do this. This is all that remains of a part of me. One third of me. How the fuck am I supposed to keep functioning? How the fuck am I supposed to go on without him? How the fuck am I supposed to say anything?

Suddenly Mel's hand covers mine on the can. The simple gesture blankets me with enough momentary comfort to speak. "You know, you were a pain in the ass Middle Man. You always had to be the first to do something. Always figured it was your way of making up for not being able to be born first. You were so impatient to do everything first you were only born thirty seconds after me. Barely gave mom time to stop pushing." A small pause comes before I finish. "And now you're first of us three to leave. Of all the things I wished you weren't in a hurry to do, this was definitely it. Um...hug the rest of McCoys for me and I promise to keep watch over these down here if you keep watch over the ones up there...."

I give the can two taps and nod at Mel. As if she's practiced, she instantly says, "I'm sorry Daniel for everything. I will spend the rest of my life making it up to you and your brother. You enjoy the real Eden."

She prepares to pass the can without tapping, so I stop her. "McCoy tradition. One tap on the car door carrying the new born for safe passage into this world and two taps on the casket for safe passage out."

One of my grandfathers started it and we've kept it alive ever since. Don't worry. You can tap the can too.

With new tears, Mel taps the can twice and passes it to Destin.

Death changes peoples. I fucking know that. What I'm afraid of is the change it's making to him. You know Madden is as cold as he always is. Knox is following in his footsteps insisting to be the rock of this family while I'm keeping my head a float thanks to Mel. Any time she senses I'm drowning in my own thoughts, she lets me drown in her body instead. Whisks me away to focus on the aspects of life that are worth living for. We're each other's antidotes now. No masks for us to hide under. It's amazing. But I'm still worried as fuck. Destin's not the same brother I left. I don't even see traces of him. Honestly? I'm scared that I might lose him next. Don't fucking let me.

"You taught me my first bike trick. Taught me the technique to getting Drew to take the fall and the secret to pissing Madden off. You were always the teacher because like Drew said, you wanted to do everything first. Just don't be the first one to get kicked out of Heaven...I'm sure dad and the others will keep you in check. Look out for us down here. We fucking need it."

We fucking do.

Destin gives a double tap and passes it to Krissy. She sniffles, "I'll miss your stunt videos almost as much as your cocky smile."

She hits it twice and passes it to Vinnie.

Vinnie, Krissy, and Shelby are extended family. Vinnie was closest to Merrick, but he's always helped the rest of us when we needed it. He coordinates street races, helps move drugs sometimes, and launders money. He's kind of a jack of all trades. Daniel used him most when he wanted get paid for doing his bike tricks or when he wanted to race for high cash.

"I'll make sure to run the circuit one more time. Just for you McCoy."

He double taps and hands it to Shelby. "Pool parties won't be the same without you. We will have one more toast for you McCoy. And you have one up there for us."

Her words cause the air in my lungs to seep out. My body starts to sway, but Mel instantly holds me closer.

Aunt Kelli takes the can. Her tears hit the top and the air that just returned to my body is choked out again. "You were always up for trouble Daniel. Rest now..."

She pats it twice and hands it to Knox. With a small sob she says, "Goddamn you McCoys. When I get up there I'm kicking your ass for making me spend so much money in waterproof mascara." A small smiles comes to her somber face. "I'll make sure Triple D doesn't fall apart without you."

Two taps and she passes it to Madden who clutches it so tight I'm afraid he's going to crush the can. In a very quiet voice he states, "I'll see you sooner than you think."

What the fuck do you think he means by that?

He gives the can the farewell taps and places it in the hole. Effortlessly he tosses dirt in the grave. Unable to watch the sight, I turn my head, close my eyes, and rest it against Mel's. Holding me tightly in silence, I try to settle my spinning thoughts knowing the goodbye isn't over yet.

There's a slight bump of my shoulder which opens my eyes. Destin makes a head motion to start that way. Turning to follow him back the way we came, my ears zone in on the only two people speaking.

Madden pleads, "Aunt Kelli-"

"Don't," she harshly whispers. "You let another McCoy *die*. I hope you're right. I hope you're next." In disbelief she said that, I glance over my shoulder. "At least then, the others might have a real chance at surviving."

For the first time I can remember, Madden's jaw trembles as his steps falter. Thankfully Knox swoops in beside him, putting an arm around him, even though he tries to shrug her away. I turn back around and press my lips together.

She was out of fucking line for that, right? It's not his fault Middle Man is dead or any of them for that matter. It's The Devil's fault my brothers are in the ground. He's gonna more than pay. The streets will run with his blood. Guaranteed.

In the front of the house, I kiss Mel on the cheek. She sighs, "Be safe."

"Promise."

Mel smiles softly.

Backing away from her just as the others join her side, I walk across to my bike and put on my helmet. Once it's on, I climb on mine as Destin does his. The two of us rev them up and pull onto the empty road that rarely sees people other than us. With focus filled with dedication, we peel off down the road in opposite directions. A good distance from each other, we spin ourselves around in burnouts, leaving identical marks on the road, and head back toward each other, popping wheelies along the way. When we're close to passing one another we each let go of our bars and briefly fist bump, our final solute to our brother, a silent solid statement said with the language he understood the best. Adrenaline.

Epilogue

Melody

"I can't believe it's Christmas," I coo from beside Drew who is still half asleep.

"It happens every year," he playfully replies. Pulling me on top of him, he lifts his eyebrows, "You know what happens every morning?"

Giggling I lightly hit his chest. "It can *not* happen every morning..."

He frowns. "We don't talk like that on Christmas."

He's such a mess. A beautiful tattooed motorcycle racing mess.

I laugh again and he leans up planting a warm kiss on my lips. His hands drift down my back softly before wandering around to my boob that he lightly touches. A shudder escapes me. He growls. The kiss deepens when it should've been lightening. I let myself get lost in him for just a moment longer.

Finally I pull away and sigh, "Merry Christmas, Drew McCoy."

He rocks his hard on against my body that's aching for it to be inside. "It could be an even merrier Christmas."

I shake my head slowly. "I'm trying to have a real moment here."

"So am I..." When I give him a stern look he folds his hands behind his head. "Sorry. What were you saying?"

"It's Christmas," I start again. "I haven't been able to celebrate in...well since..." Memories of my mother flash in my mind. Suddenly Drew's hand strokes my cheek. "But I get to spend Christmas with you. And the rest of the family. I'm just...I'm just really grateful is all."

"Me too baby," he lightly strokes my face again. "I'd be even more grateful if we didn't have to have dinner with The Commissioner tonight."

"That is a little weird."

"Tell me about it," he grumbles. "But...he did help keep the love of my life alive, so if that's the one favor he wants from us then so be it."

He kept his word. I stayed off The Devil's radar. We met in secret with Drew escorting me of course where I recorded my testimony. Signed statements. Drew also made as many as he could. Both of us failed to mention anything about Omar. We knew if The Devil didn't kill him, he had a chance to disappear without being found on criminal charges. Somehow he managed to slip away unlike Nina who ended up dead shortly after I was supposed to. I hope Omar's safe on an island somewhere sipping mojitos with a topless blonde. Omar saved me. He saved Drew. He tried to save Daniel...he deserves that. However, with The Devil dead now, I can return to a more normal lifestyle whatever that may be. For the last couple of months, I've spent a lot of times shut in the McCoy's apartment, which wasn't terrible at all. Hanging out with Knox and Madden, Destin and Azura has been more life than I've had in years. At night, so I won't go stir crazy, Drew takes me for a bike ride. More often than not we have to stop to have sex somewhere. I can't help it! There's something so sexy about being on the bike with him! Does this make me a biker babe now?

"Speaking of the love of my life." Drew pushes my hair behind my ear. "I can't wait to put your Christmas present outside."

"It is pretty amazing..." I compliment.

We agreed a good way for him to start coping with the deaths of his brothers outside of helping to take down of The Devil, was for him to keep sculpting. We also agreed, I needed a new Eden, not just because I destroyed the last one with the fail safe I had installed, but because I really enjoyed gardening. So we created a garden around the back where I grow veggies, herbs, and flowers. Nothing that can kill and just a few things that can heal. For Christmas, Drew made a sculpture of both of our hands folded together to go in the middle of it. He spends a lot of time out there with me, just watching, I assume trying to calm his racing mind when all else fails. It's our own little sanctuary.

"That's because *I'm* pretty amazing," he says in such a cocky way I can't help but smile. "In fact...why don't I show you how amazing I am and give you another reason to enjoy Christmas morning?"

Before I can argue his cock nestles it's way inside, a warm moan falling from my lips.

You know, I may not know what the future holds for me as a whole, but I know the most important part. I got what I've always wanted. I've finally got what I wished for for Christmas all those years ago. I have a family now. A big one. One I've risked my life to protect and one that any time it's necessary I'll risk it again. Because life's about the choices you chose for the people you love. Not the mistakes you make. Not the masks you wear. Not the broken promises. At the end of it all, it's about the family you choose to protect and the family that chooses to protect you. Choose wisely. I did.

THANK YOUS

Crazy Lady- I love you, lol that's all this time.

Her Husband- Thank you for caring for me in your own special way.

The Law Student- You're my sister. I love you lots.

The Lumberjack- It's hard to say thank you the way I want to so just know, you really do have a place nestled in my heart no matter what the future brings.

Nanny Job- Some day when the kids are old enough they'll love these books, lol

Sissy B- Glad you're in our family. Most def.

Katniss- I love that we never have to apologize for our schedules. I do hope they start to sync up again. Fo' real! lol

The Real Life Erin- Ride or Die. Enough said.

Throwback- Love all you do for me, the team, my career and life. You are an amazing woman.

The PAs- Left and Right brain, thanks for watching out over me when I can't even do it for myself. Love you.

The Editor- I love hugging you! You are more amazing in person, which I didn't think would be possible, but it is. Hopefully you stay addicted to my books and wanna keep working with me for um....forever? Lol

Boss Lady- I just wanna keep you! Like move to the south so I can, please. Pretty please? Lol fine, fine, but you have such a magical energy around you, I just wanna be around it all the time. Thank you for giving me the chances you have to be in your life and your company.

Genie- The world is finally seeing your magic. Keep sparkling.

To the writer's I admire- The list changes and grows every day, but here is my special thank you to all of you. You are wonderful.

Dream Team- You Rock! Thanks for being there. Being understanding. For being family...

Sophie L- You are such a doll. You are a major supporter and I know it and can't thank you enough for it. You are on the list for reasons to go to Florida...

Tara M- You're practically family. You have been since day one. I know we're far but like I said, I'm always here for you just like you are for me. Tell book club 'hey hey hey' from me!

Bloggers- Every time you answer a message or a request for me or for others you give this industry hope for indies. Thank you!

Readers- Last, but never least. You are the reason the voices have an audience. I thank you for that. I thank you for the years of dreaming come true. Thank you for staying with me and riding the waves. (Thanks for the reviews too!)

Until next time....

Curious about what happens to the Merrick McCoy?

Make sure you check out his books:

Classic

Vintage

Masterpiece

Wondering about The Devil's death?

Curious if Knox and Madden end up together?

Make sure you keep an eye out for The Adrenaline Series Standalones!

Up next is Destin McCoy in "Error".

COMING SOON!

More by Xavier Neal

Senses Series:
Vital (Prequel) Found in Interwoven
Blind (Book 1)
Deaf (Book 2
Numb (Book 3)
Hush (Book 4)
Savor (Book 5)
Callous (Book 6)
Agonize (Book 7)
Suffocate (Book 8)
Mollify (Book 9)
Senses Series Box Set (Books 1-5)

Havoc Series
Havoc (Book 1)
Chaos (Book 2)
Insanity (Book 3)
Collapse (Book 4)
Devastate (Book 5)
Havoc Series Box Set (Books 1-3)

Never Say Neverland
Get Lost
Lost in Lies
Lies Mistrust and Fairy Dust (Coming Soon)

Adrenaline Series
Classic
Vintage (Coming Soon)
Masterpiece (Coming Soon)

Connect with Xavier Neal

Links: www.xavierneal.com

Facebook: https://www.facebook.com/XavierNealAuthorPage

Twitter: @XavierNeal87

Goodreads:https://www.goodreads.com/author/show/4990135.Xavier_Neal

Interested in joining my newsletter so you don't miss a thing? Send me a quick email with your email address to be added!

Follow Entetwine Publishing for more great books
Facebook: www.facebook.com/Entertwinepub
Twitter: @Entertwine1
Goodreads:https://www.goodreads.com/user/show/34469714-
entertwine-publishing
Or join our mailing list. Sign up is easy and we never share or sell
your information. You will receive monthly newsletters debuting
new covers, upcoming releases, author interviews and more. Sign up
here: http://goo.gl/forms/bwQuKcxSFr

Made in the USA
Columbia, SC
04 July 2018